The Prophecy

EL DORADO COUNTY LIBRARY
345 FAIR LANE
PLACERVILLE, CA 95667

Look for other ANIMORPHS®
titles by K.A. Applegate:

#1 The Invasion
#2 The Visitor
#3 The Encounter
#4 The Message
#5 The Predator
#6 The Capture
#7 The Stranger
#8 The Alien
#9 The Secret
#10 The Android
#11 The Forgotten
#12 The Reaction
#13 The Change
#14 The Unknown
#15 The Escape
#16 The Warning
#17 The Underground
#18 The Decision
#19 The Departure
#20 The Discovery
#21 The Threat
#22 The Solution
#23 The Pretender
#24 The Suspicion
#25 The Extreme
#26 The Attack
#27 The Exposed
#28 The Experiment
#29 The Sickness
#30 The Reunion
#31 The Conspiracy
#32 The Separation
#33 The Illusion

<MEGAMORPHS>

#1 The Andalite's Gift
#2 In the Time of Dinosaurs
#3 Elfangor's Secret

The Hork-Bajir Chronicles

ALTERNAMORPHS

The First Journey

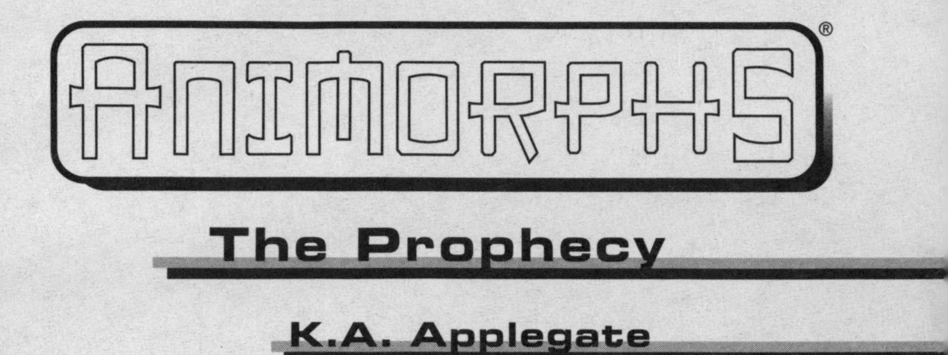

SCHOLASTIC INC.
New York Toronto London Auckland Sydney
Mexico City New Delhi Hong Kong

Cover illustration by David B. Mattingly
Art Direction/Design by Karen Hudson

If you purchased this book without a cover, you should be aware that this book is stolen property. It was reported as "unsold and destroyed" to the publisher, and neither the author nor the publisher has received any payment for this "stripped book."

No part of this publication may be reproduced in whole or in part, or stored in a retrieval system, or transmitted in any form or by any means, electronic, mechanical, photocopying, recording, or otherwise, without written permission of the publisher. For information regarding permission, write to Scholastic Inc., Attention: Permissions Department, 555 Broadway, New York, NY 10012.

ISBN 0-439-07034-1

Copyright © 1999 by Katherine Applegate.
All rights reserved. Published by Scholastic Inc.
SCHOLASTIC, ANIMORPHS, APPLE PAPERBACKS and associated logos are trademarks and/or registered trademarks of Scholastic Inc.

10 9 8 7 6 5 4 3 2 1 9/9 0 1 2 3 4/0

Printed in the U.S.A.
First Scholastic printing, October 1999

The author wishes to thank Melinda Metz for her assistance in preparing this manuscript.

For Michael and Jake

The Prophecy

CHAPTER 1

My name is Cassie.

Just Cassie. At least that's all I'm going to tell you. It's not because I think I'm so special I only need one name. I know I'm not Jewel or Brandy or Beck.

I'm actually pretty ordinary. If you saw me walking down one of the halls at your school, you probably wouldn't give me a second look. Unless it was one of the days when I had a little bird poop on my jeans from working with my dad in his Wildlife Rehabilitation Clinic. If it was a bird-poop day, you might give me a second "oh-gross" look.

But I really am your basic, average girl. A first and last name plus middle initial kind of girl. Ex-

cept for the fact that I spend most of my time trying to stop the Yeerk invasion of Earth.

That's why I can only tell you my first name. If the Yeerks knew my last name, I'd be dead. No, worse than dead.

Let me give you the Cliffs Notes version.

Fact: Yeerks are alien parasites that have the appearance of small gray slugs. They enter their hosts through the ear canal, then spread their soft bodies into the crevices of their hosts' brains.

Fact: The Yeerks have already enslaved many species, including the Hork-Bajir, the Gedds, and the Taxxons, although the Taxxons submitted willingly. Now the Yeerks have targeted the entire human race for use as hosts.

Fact: You already know someone who is controlled by a Yeerk. You just don't know you know someone who is controlled by a Yeerk. Yeerks can access their hosts' memories and make them act exactly the way they always have. A human host, called a Controller, cannot move a single muscle unless the Yeerk in his or her head gives the order.

Fact: The Animorphs may be your only hope of escaping becoming a human-Controller yourself.

The Animorphs are me and four of my friends — Jake, Rachel, Marco, and Tobias. A great Andalite prince named Elfangor gave us the power to morph into animals. He knew he was about to die, and he didn't want to leave Earth completely defenseless against the Yeerks. Later we were joined in our fight by Elfangor's younger brother, Ax. Aximili-Esgarrouth-Isthill.

Usually the six of us work as a team, but tonight I had a secret mission, and I didn't want too many people around. I asked Rachel if she'd be my backup, and of course she agreed.

You should see Rachel. She's like Stone Cold Steve Austin crossed with Miss Teen USA. Unlike me, Rachel is someone who could pull off the whole I'm-so-special-I-only-need-one-name deal even if she didn't have to keep her identity a secret.

"So are we going in or what?" Rachel asked me.

I stared up at the old Victorian house. A single light burned in one window. A loose shutter kept swinging back and forth on its hinges. The screeching sound made the hair at the back of my neck prickle.

"We're going in," I answered, ignoring the prickling sensation.

"This plan of yours is . . . what's the word I'm looking for?" Rachel asked. "Oh, yeah. Insane. As in Looney Toeowww —"

Rachel's words turned into a high meow. Her vocal cords had started to change first.

"We have to do this," I told her as her nose narrowed and sprouted fur. "It's life and death."

I watched Rachel for a few more moments. She was going to use her cat morph to go into the house. I was going to use my rat morph. I figured it couldn't hurt to give her a little head start. That way she'd be in total control of her cat brain before I became all small and delicious.

When a fluffy black-and-white tail sprang out of Rachel's rear, I decided I'd waited long enough. I focused on the rat DNA inside me, and instantly felt my hands begin to wither.

Morphing is easier for me than anyone else in the group. Maybe it's because I spend so much time around animals. I don't know.

But even for me, morphing isn't a smooth transformation. It's not like my body shrinks first, then grows hair, then shoots out whiskers and a tail.

No, morphing is a lot less logical than that. Grosser, too. Like right now I had little tiny hands, and I could feel coarse hair popping out on my back. But otherwise, I still looked like me.

Then my ears rolled up to the top of my head, and my eyeballs contracted until they were the size of BBs. I felt a sloshing, twisting sensation as my internal organs began to shift and shrink.

My nose and mouth stretched, merged, then re-formed. My teeth sharpened. A wave of dizziness engulfed me as I fell toward the ground, my body shrinking to the size of a . . . of a rat. My hairless, ropey tail appeared and I was done.

<Dog door by the porch, but the dog pee smells in the yard are stale,> Rachel announced in thought-speak.

My little rat heart was racing. My little rat brain was ordering me to run, run, run away from the cat. I clamped down on my new instincts. It's easier when you've already morphed a particular animal before, as I had done with the rat. The first time can be tough, though.

<After you,> I answered.

Rachel took off across the lawn, her body low to the ground. I scurried behind her. The grass brushed up against my belly and tickled my nose.

Without a sound, Rachel slipped through the dog door. <You could have held it open for me,> I complained. I gave the door a head butt. It opened wide enough for me to scramble through.

<There was only one light on,> I reminded Rachel. <Upstairs. Left. Let's try there first.>

We beat feet to the staircase. It would take me forever to haul myself up all those stairs. I decided to take the rat ramp instead. I dug my

claws into the wood and climbed the side of the banister. Then I ran straight up.

Of course, Rachel still got to the top before me. I half-climbed, half-fell off the banister and followed her down the hall to the lighted room. I hoped we hadn't gotten here too late.

I took a quick peek inside. Yes! My math teacher was sitting at a desk grading papers. At least I knew this was the right place.

I ducked back. <We have to wait until —>

EEEEEEE!

<She saw us!> Rachel cried. <Get out! Now!>

<That wasn't her,> I shot back. <Teakettle. She'll be coming out. Hide!>

I pressed myself tight against the wall. I squeezed my eyes shut tight so she wouldn't see them glistening in the shadows.

I felt the floor begin to vibrate. Did she see me? Did she see me?

No. Her big feet walked right on by.

<Now's our chance,> Rachel said. <Let's do it!> She darted into the room and leaped up onto the desk. <What am I looking for exactly?>

<A doodle. It's, um, of a . . . a heart,> I stammered. I tried to climb up the desk leg. But it was metal. My claws couldn't get a grip.

<Think I see it,> Rachel answered. <If the heart has "Cassie Loves Jake" printed in the

middle with a really dorky cupid drawn next to it.>

<That's it. I accidentally turned it in with my test. Just get it. And don't say anything,> I warned Rachel.

<Nothing?>

<Nothing! Not. One. Word.>

Rachel laughed and leaped down off the desk with the sheet of paper in her teeth. <Okay, you're my best friend. So not one word. Especially not "Awww, isn't that sweet?" And definitely not "Cassie is in lo-ove, Cassie is in lo-ove." And no way I'd ever say —>

<I knew I should have done this alone.>

CHAPTER 2

The cool night air fluttered my owl feathers as I flapped toward home. I tightened my right talon around the doodle. There was no way I was going to lose it again.

I still couldn't believe I'd turned it in to a teacher. Was love turning my brain to mush, or what? I wondered if Jake ever did stupid stuff because he was daydreaming about me.

We never talked about things like that. We'd never even used the "L" word to each other. That's what Rachel calls it. The "L" word.

But even though he'd never said it out loud, I knew that Jake loved me. And I knew Jake knew I loved him, even though I'd never said it out loud, either.

That was totally clear when we kissed. Yes, even though we don't walk around groping each other like some couples, we have kissed a few times. Usually right after we've managed to survive something horrible. It's usually an "I-can't-believe-we're-alive!" kiss.

Not that I'm complaining. Well, not exactly. I have to admit it would be nice to kiss Jake after a movie instead of after a battle or some other near-death experience.

I dropped one wing and made a sharp turn. The back of our barn came into sight.

Hork-Bajir!

The distinctive nightmare shape moved through the shadows that were bright as day to me. Just one. One was enough.

Shouldn't be here! Couldn't be here! The Yeerks, they had to know everything!

No!

The image of my parents being ripped to bits by the Hork-Bajir's blades blasted into my brain. Images of other Yeerks rounding up my friends. Doors kicked in, Dracon beams firing, flashing blades. Rachel. Jake.

No! NO!

Couldn't worry about them. Not now. Focus! Had to stop this one Hork-Bajir. Just this one. Then . . .

Land on the other side of the barn, demorph, then morph to wolf, attack, attack!

No time. It would take too long. Too late! The Hork-Bajir could . . . what was a lone Hork-Bajir doing here? One by himself? Irrelevant! Focus!

What would Rachel do? Attack right now. She wouldn't wait to morph. She'd swoop down and rake the Hork-Bajir with her talons.

Attack now.

I focused on the Hork-Bajir and flew straight for it. I'd aim for the eyes. While it was staggering around blind, I'd morph from owl to human to wolf. Or polar bear. Then I'd go for the throat. I could almost taste the flesh already.

Closer. Closer. I stretched out my talons, preparing to strike. A noiseless night-stalker designed by nature for much smaller prey.

I flew between the light above the shed and the Hork-Bajir. The Hork-Bajir spun, alerted by my shadow. He would slice me in half!

Then, in the light, at the last possible moment . . .

<Aaaahhh!>

I jerked my talons back and spun my body hard to the left. I crash-landed in the dirt a few feet away from the Hork-Bajir. I wasn't hurt but I was definitely shaking.

I lay there on my side in the dirt, a wing crumpled beneath me. <Hi, Jara Hamee,> I said. <Lovely night for a walk.>

This Hork-Bajir wasn't a Controller, wasn't a creature of the Yeerks. It was Jara Hamee, one of the tiny group of free Hork-Bajir. I'd almost blinded him. The thought made me nauseous.

But my entire universe was being put back in place in my mind now. No attack on my parents. The Yeerks did not know about us. No violent assault to seize Jake and Rachel, Ax and Tobias and Marco.

None of that was happening. And eventually my heart would stop hammering like it was trying to get out of my rib cage.

I concentrated on my own DNA and demorphed as fast as I could. <What are you doing here, Jara? It's too dangerous for you to be away from your valley.>

The colony of free Hork-Bajir live in a hidden valley created for them by a being called the Ellimist. Even if you know exactly where it is, it's hard to find. Your eyes just seem to slide away from it. Your mind just seems to want to forget it. It's the only place that the Hork-Bajir are at all safe from the Yeerks. Or from humans for that matter. Most humans who saw a Hork-Bajir would shoot first, ask questions later. It's not hard to understand why. The Hork-Bajir look as if they were designed to kill. But they are among the gentlest creatures I've ever encountered.

They're even vegetarians. The razor-sharp blades on their ankles, knees, wrists, and elbows are for stripping bark off trees. That's what they eat. Bark.

"Need help," Jara answered. "Toby say, 'Father, get human friends. Bring.'"

I emerged into fully human form. "Why? What happened? What's wrong?" I demanded. Amazing how now my human heart was still beating way too fast from the adrenaline rush of sheer terror.

Jara rocked back and forth on his big T. Rex feet. "Alien come valley."

"The Yeerks? They found you?!" I cried. "Did they attack you? What's the situation?"

Talking to Jara Hamee was sort of like talking to a four-year-old. Which was fine usually. But not now. Every second wasted could be putting the free Hork-Bajir in danger.

"Not Yeerks," Jara explained. "Arn. From the old world. Arn . . . make . . . Hork-Bajir."

CHAPTER 3

<An Arn, on Earth? Here? Why? That's the question. What's he up to?> Rachel wondered.

<He had to come. *Star Wars: The Phantom Menace* isn't coming out on DVD there for, like, two years. He buys up a bunch of copies here, takes 'em home, makes a fortune.>

<Good grief, Marco, you live science fiction, why do you want to *watch* science fiction?>

<Don't be dissing TPM,> Marco said. <Cool is cool.>

The whole group was in bird-of-prey morph. It was the fastest way to get to the Hork-Bajir valley. The night had passed. The sun had come up on a new day. A beautiful, cool Saturday morn-

ing. The deep green forest foothills below us, the towering cumulus above. It was almost hot in the direct sunlight, cooler under the shadow of the Mount Everest-sized clouds.

<If he's hoping to pick up some new slaves in the colony, he can forget it,> Rachel continued. <The Hork-Bajir are never going to be Arn slaves again. We'll see to that.>

Rachel wasn't being totally accurate. The Hork-Bajir were never slaves on their home planet. Not exactly. It's not like the Arn made the Hork-Bajir wait on them hand and foot.

What we knew of all this came from Tobias, who'd heard the story from Jara Hamee. There was a terrible cataclysm on the planet we call the Hork-Bajir home world, but in those days the planet was populated only by the Arn. It shattered the planet's crust and stripped away much of the atmosphere. The Arn who survived needed trees to provide oxygen. Lots of exceedingly large trees. They didn't feel like taking care of the trees themselves. Solution? They used genetic engineering to design creatures of low intelligence who ate tree bark: the Hork-Bajir.

An elegantly simple solution for the Arn who were masters of genetic manipulation.

The Hork-Bajir just lived their lives, utterly unaware that the Arn even existed deep down in the impossibly steep valleys. They took care of the trees they depended on for food. They did what came naturally. Did what the Arn designed them to do.

Then came the Yeerks.

The Yeerks didn't see tree maintenance workers when they saw the Hork-Bajir. They saw an army. They made the Hork-Bajir their hosts. They took the peaceful creatures away from their home planet and began using them as killing machines, shock troops of the Yeerk Empire.

There's a longer story there, but that's the short version.

<Rachel, you know, there are some nice thermals today, we have a sweet little tailwind,> Tobias said. <You don't have to exhaust yourself with all that flapping.>

Tobias is the expert. Tobias is, or was, trapped in red-tailed hawk morph. He regained his ability to morph, but he's chosen to consider hawk as his true body.

Long story there, too.

I stretched open my wings and caught one of those thermals. The warm air lifted up my osprey body.

A couple of thermals later I spotted about twenty Hork-Bajir clustered together in the center of the valley. Adults and kids. Seeing the kids was especially cool. They were the first Hork-Bajir in generations to be born into freedom.

We circled down from the clouds and landed, one by one. All of us demorphed, except Tobias.

Toby Hamee moved away from the group to greet us. Toby is the daughter of Jara Hamee and Ket Halpak. She's what the Hork-Bajir call "different." She's what the Arn call a freak of nature. She is a seer. A Hork-Bajir whose intelligence matches that of the Arn themselves.

"Thank you for coming. We felt the need of your advice."

"No problemo," Marco said. "It was either this or wash my dad's car."

"The Arn landed last evening in a small Yeerk ship. We nearly killed him, thinking he was a Controller. He has some sort of plan in mind. We told him to wait so we could bring you to advise us."

"We're flattered," Jake said, "but you don't need us."

"I do need you," Toby said. "I especially need you," she added, looking at Ax. "If I understand his goal, we could use an Andalite's opinion."

"Let's see what he's got to say," Jake said.

We followed Toby over to the Hork-Bajir. They moved closer together to make room for us in the circle.

The Arn stood in the center. The first thing I noticed about him was his eyes. They glittered like diamonds lit from within. Their intensity dazzled me.

I blinked a few times, and began to take in more details of the Arn's appearance. He had four legs, two elongated arms, and a pair of short wings. He was about half as tall as Ax and his skin was a vibrant emerald-green.

I stared at the Arn. We'd gotten almost used to seeing alien races: Hork-Bajir, Taxxons, Andalites, Howlers. Almost. There was still something unsettling about seeing something, someone who was so definitely not from around here.

And even by the standards of aliens, the Arn was bizarre. He stood, surrounded by seven-foot-tall nightmares, watched by a deceptively peaceful-looking Andalite, a hawk, and a gaggle of badly dressed kids.

And he was still the strangest being there. And all the more strange to me because I could see, or felt I could see, a deep, unreachable sadness behind those glittering, unhuman eyes.

"These are humans," the Arn said, nodding. "Yes. I spent a day waiting in orbit, learning your languages. You have many interesting languages but your biology is not at all remarkable, I'm afraid. Two arms, two legs, a most unstable platform. And entirely lacking in physical innovation: simple bilateral symmetry for the most part."

"Yeah, nice to meet you, too," Rachel said. "What are you up to, what do you want?"

"I am Arn."

<We know about the Arn,> Tobias said. <We know your species.>

If the glittery-eyed creature was shocked at being addressed by a bird he didn't show it.

"I am Quafijinivon," he said. "The species you claim to know is no more. And I am the last of the Arn.

CHAPTER 4

"I have come to give the Hork-Bajir a chance for freedom and rebirth. And revenge against the Yeerks. I have a plan that will require your assistance."

"Who's going to give them a shot at revenge against you, Arn?" Rachel muttered.

"Ten bucks says whatever he has in mind ends up with us screaming and running," Marco said.

Quafijinivon's small red mouth pursed disapprovingly. "I have very little time, humans. No time at all for pleasantries. I will live for only four hundred and twelve more days, give or take a few hours, that is a biological fact."

<There are forces other than biology,> Ax

said. He gave his deadly tail just the slightest little twitch.

"Yes, well, an Andalite. Charming, as always." He made a grimace that might have been a smile. "Recently I intercepted a Yeerk transmission and learned to my amazement that a free Hork-Bajir colony existed on Earth. I risked everything to steal a Yeerk ship, and have traveled a great distance to find —"

"Do the Yeerks know the location of the colony?" Jake interrupted.

"No," Quafijinivon answered. "I found it myself. We Arn long ago developed technology to track our —"

"What exactly is this plan of yours?" Rachel demanded.

The Arn shot her a quelling look, clearly displeased to have been interrupted a second time. "My plan is to collect samples of the DNA of the free Hork-Bajir. With their permission," he added quickly. "I would then use the DNA to create a new colony on my home planet."

<To do what? Fight the Yeerks for you?> Tobias asked. He edged back and forth on the log he was using as a perch. <Is that what you meant when you said the Hork-Bajir would get revenge?>

I could practically feel the disapproval coming off him. Tobias is probably closer to the Hork-

Bajir than any of the rest of us. Toby Hamee is named after him. Toby for Tobias.

"To fight the Yeerks, yes," Quafijinivon replied. "But not for me. To regain their planet. To regain what the Yeerks took from them."

And from you, I thought. I'm usually pretty good at figuring out people's motives. But I wasn't sure what the Arn's deal was yet. Was he trying to help the Hork-Bajir? Or was he just trying somehow to help himself?

Jake shook his head. "Even if the Hork-Bajir agreed, how would some small colony win a war against the Yeerks? No ships. No orbital weapons platforms. Not even handheld Dracon beams."

"Yeah, the Yeerks have these cute little things called weapons," Marco added.

"So would the Hork-Bajir," Quafijinivon answered. "Before they lost their lives to the Yeerks, Aldrea-Iskillion-Falan and Dak Hamee stole an entire transport ship filled with handheld Dracon beams, as well as a good supply of very sophisticated explosives."

I saw Jake and Marco exchange a look.

Marco shrugged. "No question that opening a new front against the Yeerks would be helpful. A guerilla war on the Hork-Bajir home world would pull Yeerk resources away from Earth, away from the Andalites."

"This isn't our fight," I pointed out. I nodded

toward Jara Hamee and Toby. "I think we're just here to advise."

Jake winced, realizing he'd been playing boss.

"I will do whatever I can to continue the work of Aldrea and Dak Hamee," Toby said guardedly. "A DNA sample is little enough to ask."

Aldrea and Dak were Toby's great-grandparents. They were heroes to the Hork-Bajir because they had led the battle against the Yeerks. And lost their lives in the fight.

"I give, too," Jara answered.

The other Hork-Bajir all chimed in. All agreeing to allow Quafijinivon to harvest their DNA, despite the fact that none of them besides Toby had any idea what DNA was.

Quafijinivon lowered his head. "I thank you," he told them. "But that is only the beginning. There is one more thing I must ask before I can move forward with my plan."

"Uh-oh," Marco said in a loud stage whisper. "Here it comes."

The Arn turned his weird eyes toward me and the other Animorphs. "Aldrea and Dak Hamee hid the weapons. I have been unable to recover them. We Arn are perhaps unequaled in our biological science. But we have no great technological skill."

<So what do you propose?> Ax asked. <Do you plan to create new Hork-Bajir and send them out to search for the weapons?>

"No. That would be self-defeating. I have something rather more . . . unusual in mind."

<Unusual is our middle name,> Tobias said dryly.

"I have in my possession the *Ixcila* of Aldrea-Iskillion-Falan."

<Seerow's daughter?> Ax exclaimed.

"Ixcila?" Jake repeated.

"Her stored persona," Quafijinivon explained impatiently. "Her brain wave patterns. Her memories. Her personality. Her essence."

His voice had started to sound quavery, and for the first time I realized that he was old and weak. It's impossible to tell the age of an alien till you know what to look for.

"The *Atafalxical* must be performed. It is the only way to unlock the *Ixcila.* But the Ceremony of Rebirth will not succeed unless there is a strong receptacle mind available, a mind as strong as Aldrea's own."

Receptacle mind. The phrase repeated itself in my head until it became nothing more than a jumble of sounds. An echo that felt important but whose meaning I could not grasp.

I felt that something-crawling-up-your-neck sensation that warns of disaster approaching. The tornado is coming, Auntie Em.

"If all goes well, the *Ixcila* will move into the receptacle mind, and we will be able to com-

municate with Aldrea," Quafijinivon continued. "She will be able to lead us to the weapons."

"And what happens to the receptacle?" Jake asked.

"Oh, it will be undamaged, if that is what concerns you," Quafijinivon answered. "The receptacle mind simply shares space with the *Ixcila* until the *Ixcila* is returned to storage."

The Arn pulled in a wheezing breath. "Only one in four Ceremonies are actually completed. The appropriate receptacle mind is essential. Aldrea's *Ixcila* will be attracted to someone most like she was. Someone strong, fierce, independent. Presumably female. Hork-Bajir or Andalite, most likely, but I suppose she might gravitate toward a human. If such a human female existed."

"Oh, I think I know where one could be found," Marco said.

CHAPTER 5

"And the next words out of Rachel's mouth will be . . ."

"I'll do it," Rachel said, giving Marco a self-mocking look.

"Bingo," Marco said.

"I don't consider myself worthy of the honor," Toby said, "but I, too, will volunteer."

I kept quiet. The description fit Rachel and Toby. Not me.

We debated. We argued. Rachel for. Tobias for. Ax and Marco against. Jake listening, weighing, considering whether to once more put us all in harm's way. Me? I just felt unsettled.

I knew how the debate would end. It was a

chance to hurt the Yeerks. It was a chance to help the free Hork-Bajir. A no-brainer, morally or strategically.

Except for the fact that, as Marco pointed out, it was insane. We very seldom ended up refusing to do what was insane.

Quafijinivon asked if there was some more confined space nearby. The Hork-Bajir led us to a cave.

I shivered. I told myself it was because the cave was cold.

<I would like to ask a question,> Ax said. He turned all four of his eyes toward the Arn. <You claim that the receptacle will share space with the *Ixcila* of Aldrea until it is time for it to be returned to storage.>

"That is correct," Quafijinivon answered. His eyes were as bright as stars in the darkness.

<What if Aldrea does not wish to leave the receptacle after she helps us find the weapons?> Ax asked. <Is there some way to force her to do so?>

There was a long moment of silence. The kind of silence that feels as if it sucks half the oxygen out of the air.

"Aldrea must choose to release her hold on the receptacle," Quafijinivon said, not exactly answering the question Ax had asked.

Ax rolled one eye stalk toward Rachel and one

toward Toby. We'd all agreed that Aldrea would be drawn to one of them . . . if the so-called Ceremony worked at all.

Rachel, because of her Rachelness. Toby, because she was Aldrea's great-granddaughter and a Hork-Bajir seer.

<And if she doesn't chose to release her hold?> Ax prodded.

"We could probably sell the story rights to Lifetime for big bucks," Marco commented. "This is so television for women. Two strong, independent girls. One body."

Toby turned to Ax. "You only ask this because you don't trust Aldrea. As an Andalite you mistrust anyone who would choose to permanently become Hork-Bajir," she accused.

Toby's gifts didn't just make her more articulate than the other Hork-Bajir. They made her more insightful. More capable of drawing conclusions.

I wondered if she was right about Ax. The thought of an Andalite choosing to become Hork-Bajir had to be repellent to Ax. Almost sacrilegious. Andalites are not known for their humility.

But I understood Aldrea's choice. More than that, I admired it. I admired her. Aldrea discovered that her own fellow Andalites had created a virus targeted to kill the Hork-Bajir. It was a cold-blooded, military-minded decision. The Andalites knew they would lose the Hork-Bajir planet. They knew that if the Hork-Bajir survived in large numbers they would be used as weapons for the Yeerks. And that with such troops the Yeerks would have a much-strengthened chance of conquering other planets throughout the galaxies.

The leader of the desperate Andalite forces on the planet made the call. Later it was disavowed by the Andalite people. Too late to stop what happened. Sometimes, in war, even the "good guys" do awful things.

Once Aldrea learned of the virus, she was forced to choose between her own people and Dak Hamee, the Hork-Bajir seer she had come to love. She chose Dak. She stayed in Hork-Bajir morph until the change became permanent. Aldrea and Dak vowed to fight both the Yeerks and the Andalites. They died keeping this vow.

Ax shifted his weight from one hoof to the other. <I ask only because it is a logical question,> he finally said.

"I did not mean to sound suspicious of my Andalite friend," Toby said with no sincerity whatsoever.

<The Hork-Bajir have reason to be . . . hesitant . . . about trusting the Andalites,> Ax allowed.

Toby bowed her head graciously. Then she said, "I, too, want an answer, Arn."

Quafijinivon sighed. "If Aldrea does not choose to release her hold, there is no way to force her to do so," he confessed.

"I see. I trust my great-grandmother," Toby said firmly. "If she chooses me for this honor I will trust my freedom to her."

"Okay. Rachel? It's your call," Jake told her.

He clearly felt obligated to ask the question even though anyone who knows Rachel also knew what her answer would be.

"I still say let's do it," she said.

No surprise there. Rachel wouldn't have been Rachel if she'd said anything else.

Quafijinivon nodded. He reached into a small metallic pouch hanging from a cord around his neck and pulled out a small vial. The liquid inside glowed green.

"Isn't that what nuclear waste looks like?" Marco asked in a loud whisper.

"We gather to conduct the *Atafalxical,*" Quafijinivon began. "The Ceremony of Rebirth is an occasion for both solemnity and joy, for grieving and celebration."

"Not to mention a severe case of the willies," Marco said under his breath.

If he was close enough I would have elbowed

him. Not that it would have shut him up. Solemnity just isn't part of Marco's repertoire.

Quafijinivon continued with the ceremony as if he hadn't heard Marco. He pulled the stopper out of the vial and a wisp of vapor escaped. A moment later the inside of my nose started to burn, although I couldn't smell anything except the odor of damp cave.

"We call on Aldrea-Iskillion-Falan," Quafijinivon said. He reached into the pouch again. I squinted, trying to see what he'd removed. It looked like a small piece of metal.

It must have been some kind of catalyst, because the instant he dropped it into the vial, the liquid turned from green to a fluorescent scarlet. Its light washed over those closest to it.

Rachel's fair skin appeared to have been drenched in blood. Toby's green flesh had darkened until it was almost black.

Quafijinivon added another piece of metal to the vial. "We call on Aldrea-Iskillion-Falan," he repeated.

"Paging Stephen King," Marco said quietly. "R.L. Stine calling Stephen King with a message from Anne Rice."

The liquid in the vial thickened. It began to contract and expand.

In and out.

In and out.

My heart began to beat to the same rhythm. I could feel it in my chest and in the base of my throat. I could feel it in my ears and in my fingertips.

"We call on Aldrea-Iskillion-Falan. We call on Aldrea-Iskillion-Falan."

Quafijinivon repeated the words again and again, stamping his feet as he cried them out.

"We call on Aldrea-Iskillion-Falan." His voice grew louder. His feet stamped so hard they sent a vibration through the rock floor of the cave.

The liquid in the vial contracted and expanded faster. In and out. In and out. In and out.

My heartbeat matched the new rhythm.

"We. Call. On. Aldrea. Iskillion. Falan," Quafijinivon wailed.

"If I see one single zombie I am —"

The cave floor jerked under my feet. I stumbled forward and landed on my knees in front of the Arn.

"The receptacle has been chosen!" Quafijinivon shouted.

He reached out and put his hand on my head. "Will you accept the *Ixcila* of Aldrea-Iskillion-Falan?"

What? What? She chose me?

That couldn't be right.

"Will you accept the *Ixcila*?" Quafijinivon repeated, his voice echoing in the cave.

"No!" Jake snapped.

But there was only one answer I could give.

"Yes."

CHAPTER 6

I braced myself for . . . for what, I didn't know.

I once had a Yeerk in my head. I know the sensation of another being invading me. I know the violation of having my most private memories exposed. I know the horror of losing control over my own arms and legs and mouth. But I felt none of these things now.

"She chose Cassie?" I heard Rachel mumble. "I feel so ten minutes ago."

"May I speak to my great-grandmother now?" Toby asked eagerly. Her voice was filled with awe. She revealed none of Rachel's bemused resentment.

I swallowed, then swallowed again. My throat

felt as dry and scratchy as sandpaper. "I'm sorry, Toby. I don't think the Ceremony was —" I began. Then I realized something was different.

Have you ever been taking a test and totally blanked? You read a question. You know you know the answer. You know you memorized it when you were studying. But you can't get to it. It's like there's a wall in your brain separating you from the information.

That's how I felt now. And the wall was enormous. High and long and solid.

I was pretty sure Aldrea was on the other side of the wall. But nothing was getting through. I wasn't picking up even a fragment of a thought or a hint of an emotion. The only thing I knew was that something, some force, some bundle of sensations, some object or person was sitting inside my mind.

It was as if she was behind me, or beside me, but turning my head I couldn't see her. There but not visible. There nevertheless.

"Cassie, are you okay? What happened?" Jake asked calmly. Too calmly.

"Did the *Ixcila* take root?" Quafijinivon asked, his voice breaking. It was the first real emotion the Arn had shown. He wanted this to work. Needed it to work.

"Shhh," I said. "Please, just shhh, all of you."

I squeezed my eyes shut. I didn't want any outside stimulus right now.

"Aldrea?" I called aloud, softly, tentatively, feeling like an idiot talking to the dripping, dank cave walls.

No answer.

Aldrea! I repeated, this time silently, hoping she could hear my directed thought. *If you're there, please try to say something to me.*

No answer.

<Well, this is odd,> Tobias said. <Like a séance. All we need is a Ouija board.>

She had to be totally disoriented. I wondered if she'd been able to experience anything while she was in storage. Did she have any idea she had been taken to a planet in a different galaxy? Had she been aware that the Ceremony was taking place? Did she realize she wasn't in the vial now?

Did she know she was dead?

"Aldrea, if you can hear me, I want you to know that you're safe," I said.

"Safe as a dead person can be," Marco said.

<Who's safer than a dead person?> Tobias asked rhetorically.

"Aldrea, you're sharing my brain and body. My name is Cassie. I'm a human girl. I live on planet Earth. An Arn just performed the *Atafal* —"

<Arn?!>

Red dots exploded in front of my eyes. The question in my head was so loud and forceful it made me dizzy.

There was definitely a hole in the wall now. I could feel Aldrea's emotions coming through. Anger was the strongest.

<Where . . . what has . . . what have you done to me, Arn?> she demanded. <What have you done?>

Her voice was a noise like a chainsaw in my brain. "Ah! Ah! Ah! Aldrea, stop! Please, stop! You're hurting me!" I yelled.

Jake grabbed me around the shoulders and held me up. My knees had given way.

I felt a welling up of pain from Aldrea, an echo, and knew that my silent scream had hurt her back.

I pulled in a shaky breath.

"Did you guys hear that? Did she speak through my mouth?" I asked, confused.

"No, we just heard you," Rachel said. "At least, I guess it was you."

Bringing up the Arn was definitely not the way to win Aldrea's trust. I needed another way to reach her. Something that would get through her anger.

"Aldrea, don't say anything for a moment. Just listen. Let me explain," I said softly. When I felt her acceptance, I rushed on. "You were brought to this planet because there is a colony of free Hork-Bajir here. Your grandson, Jara Hamee, is part of the colony. So is your great-granddaughter, Toby Hamee."

I paused to receive Aldrea's reaction. I felt a swirl of too many emotions to take in. I caught traces of curiosity and disbelief, of hope, and fear, and panic. "Toby Hamee is in the cave with us," I continued. "Can you see her? You should be able to see through my eyes."

<All I see is blackness,> she answered.

I glanced around the cave. I wanted something basic to look at. I focused on Rachel's red shirt.

"Maybe you just aren't used to the way my brain gets information from my eyes," I told Aldrea. "Right now, I'm looking at something red."

I felt her concentrating. Then I felt the relief of recognition.

<Red!> Aldrea exclaimed.

I turned toward Toby. <Now I am looking at — is that her? Is that my great-granddaughter?> she interrupted.

"Yes," I answered.

I felt a strange desire to go and press my forehead against Toby's. It took me a moment to realize the desire was Aldrea's.

If Aldrea wanted to touch Toby, why shouldn't she? I started to take a step forward, but a group of rapid-fire questions from Aldrea stopped me.

<I don't understand. What year is this? Where is Dak? How did I get here? What happened to my own body?>

Her panic grew so intense that I felt sweat break out on my forehead.

"I think maybe it's time to call the Exorcist," Marco said. Not a joke, really. He was worried. Everyone was worried.

"Do you remember an old Arn storing your *Ixcila*?" I asked.

<Yes,> she replied. <I agreed to have my persona harvested, although I didn't think the Arn were really advanced enough to make a successful transplant.>

I knew the moment the knowledge hit her. Really hit her. My heart started to pound, and I felt like my nerve endings were getting jolts of electricity.

<But that is what has happened, isn't it? A successful transplant?> Aldrea continued. <This can only mean that —>

I hesitated. But she had to know the truth. "Yes, Aldrea, you are dead."

CHAPTER 7

ALDREA

My name is Aldrea-Iskillion-Falan.

And I have been told that I am dead.

Impossible.

Ridiculous.

The thought patterns the Arn had stored would only allow for a crude reproduction of me. A jumble of facts and sensations. Nothing more. There was no possibility that the thoughts and emotions I was experiencing now could be coming out of electrical impulses and chemicals collected years ago. I must have been knocked unconscious in a battle. A hallucination. A ploy the Yeerks were using to break me. They must be hoping that I —

But what about the body? What about the

hands with too few fingers to be Andalite, the arms too weak and frail to be Hork-Bajir?

I didn't want to believe I was dead. But I could not deny the fact that I was in a body that was not my own. A small, weak, defenseless body covered in furless brown skin.

"Aldrea?" the creature called Cassie said. "Are you all right?"

I realized that I wasn't just hearing her words. I was feeling bits of emotion, too. Empathy and concern and sadness. A little fear, too. Fear for herself.

<Is Dak alive?> I asked, speaking in what felt like my own native tongue of thought-speak. I had to know. Unless . . . no, either way I had to know. The emotions from Cassie gave me my answer before her words.

"No, Aldrea. He died a long time ago. A long way from here. I'm sorry," she answered.

<Where is his *Ixcila*?> I demanded. I knew he had one, too. It could be put into another body the way mine had. Dak and I could still be together.

"I don't know," she answered.

Cassie turned her gaze toward the Arn. It took me a moment to realize that she wasn't communicating with him in the way we had been communicating. It took me a few moments more to comprehend how her brain received input from her ears and how I could use her brain to translate the data into words I could understand.

"The Yeerks did extensive blasting to create level places for training grounds. My lab was heavily damaged. The *Ixcila* of Dak Hamee was destroyed," the Arn explained.

Was it true? If so, then Dak was truly dead. Dead like my parents. Like my brother, Barafin.

<Then let me die, Arn,> I said. <Let me die, too.>

Had I had the chance to say good-bye to Dak? Had we fought side by side until the end? I would never know. My *Ixcila* had been collected before my death, so the memories of my last moments with Dak did not exist.

I felt a wave of sadness from Cassie. I shoved it away. I had no use for her emotions. She was nothing to me.

There was one final question I had to ask, although I was terrified to hear the answer. <My son. What happened to the son I named after my father, Seerow?>

I waited for Cassie to repeat my question.

It was the young Hork-Bajir who answered. "They took him, Great-grandmother. Seerow became a Controller. He was brought to Earth as part of their army, here. He died in captivity."

There was not a worse fate I could have imagined for my child. The Yeerks had made his life a living death. And I had not been there to protect him.

"But Seerow's son, Jara Hamee, my father, escaped with the help of the humans here," Toby continued. "And I, your great-granddaughter, was born in freedom."

I studied her through my new eyes. There was something about her. Something familiar. The words were too well organized, the speech flowed too smoothly, the ideas . . .

Through my despair I felt a tiny bubble of something that could have been joy.

<Ask her if she's different,> I told Cassie.

A smile spread across Toby's face when she heard the question.

"Yes, Great-grandmother, I am different," she answered. "I am different as Dak Hamee was different."

A seer. A seer born in freedom.

"We have brought you back from death because we need your help," Toby said.

<Tell her that there is nothing she could ask of me that I would not give,> I said to Cassie.

My rebirth had brought me a pain that felt almost unbearable. My Dak gone. My Seerow gone.

But it had brought me a gift as well. The chance to know my great-granddaughter.

I wouldn't give that up for anything. Perhaps I would even see Toby's child one day.

CHAPTER 8

The Arn quickly outlined his plan for Aldrea. I could feel her mistrust and anger growing as he spoke.

"Can you help us?" the Arn asked. "Do you remember where the weapons are hidden?"

<No. I know nothing of any weapons. It must have occurred . . . if it did occur, after,> Aldrea said.

I repeated her message.

The Arn nodded his head sadly. "And yet, it was the mind that found the hiding place. Found once, it could find again. Could Aldrea find them?"

<Could I find weapons I hid? Yes, most likely,> Aldrea said.

"Then the two of us — no, I suppose that should be the three of us, counting the receptacle — will leave tomorrow," Quafijinivon replied. "While the new Hork-Bajir are being grown in my laboratory, you will have time to retrieve the weapons."

"If Cassie goes, we go," Jake said.

"But she is just a vessel," Quafijinivon said with a sort of greasy smile. "Why would you humans need to come?"

<Because you think she's nothing but a vessel, that's why,> Tobias said.

"I hadn't thought to bring —" Quafijinivon began.

<Tell him to be silent,> Aldrea ordered. <This discussion is pointless. I could no doubt find these weapons, but I will not help the Arn —>

<Wait, wait. You're going too fast,> I told her. I found I could communicate mind to mind with her now. As easy as any internal dialogue.

<Then let me use your speech centers. I will speak to them directly.>

A perfectly logical request. I had no real reason for refusing, did I? <If you can access my speech centers, I guess go ahead.>

Almost immediately I felt a tickling sensation in my throat. My tongue gave a twitch and I let out something that sounded way too much like a pig grunting.

"Cassie, you okay?" Rachel asked.

I couldn't answer her. Aldrea had my teeth locked together. I held up both hands and nodded, trying to show everyone that I was okay. My hands were still mine, at least.

"Thh — Thh —"

I could feel little specks of spit flicking down onto my chin. I expected to get at least a "say it, don't spray it" out of Marco, but he stayed quiet.

"Thh. Ihh. This. This. This is Althrea. Drr. Drr. Aldrea. Cass-ie is al-low-ing me to u-se h-er voice," Aldrea explained.

She reminded me of a little kid sounding out words in a book that was too hard for her. She also reminded me of a Yeerk. She was using my mouth! Speaking with my voice!

"I sa-id I wou-ld do an-y-thing to he-l-p my great-gr-and-dau-gh-ter and the Ho-r-k-Ba-ji-r," she continued. "But I wi-ll not do this."

"What do you mean?" the Arn demanded. "You must! You are refusing the chance to give the Hork-Bajirs' planet back to them?" His voice was quivering. I wasn't sure if it was because he was furious or simply exhausted.

Aldrea laughed. It was a harsh, ugly sound that hurt my throat. "No, Arn. I am refu-sing the chance to give you your planet back. That is what you are tru-ly asking. You care no-thing for the Hork-Bajir. Your kind never did."

Her words were coming much more smoothly now. Aldrea was getting comfortable with operating my mouth. I wasn't getting comfortable with letting her. I felt like the world's largest ventriloquist's dummy.

"Ridiculous," the Arn protested. "I am old. Soon I will be dead."

"You're asking me to help you use the Hork-Bajir again. Every time one of your new Hork-Bajir kills a Yeerk he will also be killing one of his own kind." Aldrea asked, "You brought me back to help Hork-Bajir kill Hork-Bajir?"

"What you say is true, Great-grandmother," Toby said. "But there is no other way. Few of our people survived the Andalite virus. Only those who had already been taken off-world by the Yeerks, and those few with natural immunity like you and my great-grandfather. We could grow again, take back our world. But not until we weaken the Yeerks."

Toby stepped up in front of me and leaned down so she could look into my eyes. No. Into Aldrea's eyes, because I might just as well not have been there. "Let me accompany you to our planet. We can start again, continue the work you and Dak Hamee began," Toby pleaded.

I felt another stab of grief from Aldrea when Toby said Dak's name. Then I felt her push that grief aside.

"You are a seer, Toby, but you are also young. You don't know what this Arn, this Andalite, and even, I suspect, these humans, intend. Even well armed, do you think the few Hork-Bajir that this creature, this Arn, this manipulator, this liar from a race of liars, this coward from a race of cowards . . ." She stabbed my finger toward the Arn. I felt my face twist into an expression of fury.

She regained control over her emotions, but now adrenaline was flooding my system. She had triggered the classic human physiological response to stress. And with that hormone rush my own fear and anger grew.

"Hork-Bajir kill Hork-Bajir and who will profit?" Aldrea demanded.

"All the enemies of the Yeerks will profit," Jake said. Toby nodded and said, "True, Great-grandmother, it would be a sideshow. It would only be a distraction for the Yeerks. Many Hork-Bajir would die. And yet we must fight."

Aldrea spread my hands wide. "Why?"

"Because we must be a free people, Great-grandmother. So far our freedom here, in this valley, on this planet, has been bought and paid for by these humans, our friends. But freedom can't be given. It must be taken and held and defended. Our freedom has to be our own creation."

I felt again some measure of Aldrea's sadness. Every word from Toby's mouth reminded her of Dak.

"Brave talk, Toby. You may reconsider when you see the bodies piled high. Your great-grandfather did."

No one said anything. The decision was Aldrea's. Had to be hers. "We go. But I warn you, Arn: You will not betray the Hork-Bajir and live. Now, let us go home."

<She calls it home,> Ax muttered.

Aldrea jerked my head toward him. <The Andalite,> she said silently to me. <What is an Andalite doing here?>

<He's a friend,> I said.

<My people were friends to the Hork-Bajir, too,> she said. Then she looked directly at Ax and, out loud, using my voice, said, "This human, Cassie, tells me you are a friend, Andalite. I warned her about Andalite friends."

<Did you warn her about Andalite *nothlits,* daughters of Seerow, who pretend to be Hork-Bajir?> Ax shot back.

<I am Hork-Bajir!>

<No. The Hork-Bajir are like Jara and Ket and the rest. You could perhaps consider yourself the equivalent of a Hork-Bajir seer, but your intelligence is not the result of a genetic fluctuation. I do not know you, Aldrea-Iskillion-Falan, but I know of you. You are highly intelligent, emotion-

ally self-controlled, capable of lying and manipulation for your own ends. You are also fundamentally peaceful, moral, courageous, and capable of self-sacrifice. You are, in short, an Andalite. Not a Hork-Bajir.>

"You could have been describing a human," Rachel said brightly. "Now, add in 'arrogant' and 'humorless,' and then you have an Andalite."

To my surprise Aldrea laughed out loud. My laugh. "Obviously you humans have spent some time with Andalites."

Ax didn't join in the sense of eased tension. He kept his large main eyes focused on me. On her.

<I want to be sure, daughter of Prince Seerow, that you realize you have only one function to perform. As soon as you show us the location of the weapons your *Ixcila* will be returned to storage. You are dead, Aldrea-Iskillion-Falan. When you have performed this one duty, this illusion of life will be ended and Cassie will be Cassie alone.>

The wall between me and Aldrea went back up. It felt even stronger than before. I had no idea what her true reaction to Ax's question was.

"I understand why the Ceremony of Rebirth was performed," she replied neutrally. "I understand that the Arn brought me here only to use me for this one purpose. I will do what I must."

Not the answer I wanted to hear.

<I will take back control of my speech centers now,> I said.

<Of course.>

A better answer. And if she'd given it without hesitation, it would have been better still.

CHAPTER 9

"Okay, we're supposed to brief you, so here goes: One of Cassie's best fighting morphs is a wolf," Rachel told Aldrea as we headed home through the sun-dappled woods.

The others had morphed and flown off ahead. At least they had been seen to fly off, and at least one no doubt did. There were plans to be made. We'd be away for a while. The Chee had to be contacted.

But if I knew Jake he'd left at least one or two others behind to watch us secretly. Jake was no happier with Aldrea's careful reply than I was.

This leisurely walk through the woods was a test. If Aldrea did anything troubling, Rachel was on hand, and probably Tobias and Ax, as well. I

didn't spot either of them. But I'd have bet anything they were close by.

Jake had suggested that Aldrea learn how to control my morphs. On the Hork-Bajir world, she'd be in charge. In a fight we needed quick responses. She needed to know which weapon to use. And we needed to see how she handled it.

"The wolf has good speed," Rachel chattered on. "Great ripping abilities with the teeth. Terrific endurance. They can run all night. Now if you'd chosen me, Aldrea, you'd have gotten some serious firepower. My African elephant morph. It's, like, fourteen thousand pounds. Not to mention my grizzly bear."

I felt a tickle of admiration mixed with amusement from Aldrea. A little of that wall between us had come back down, but what I saw and felt was only what Aldrea allowed me to see and feel.

I have to admit it's not as if I was pouring out my deepest, darkest secrets to her. I was controlling my body, my mouth, and my eyes again. But I was carefully not searching the trees and bushes for signs of Tobias or Ax, lest she figure out what I was up to.

"So, not that it bothers me, but why didn't you choose me, by the way?" Rachel burst out. "I mean, come on! There I was, all ready to go."

"Not that it bothers you," I said.

"Of course not. I'm just saying . . ."

<Why should I have chosen her?> Aldrea asked.

"She wants to know why she should have chosen you," I reported. "Should I explain to her that you are the mighty, the powerful, the ultimate Yeerk-killer, Xena: Warrior Princess, whereas I am merely an ambivalent, animal-loving, tree-hugging wuss?"

"You forget to mention that I clearly have a superior sense of style," Rachel added.

"Actually, I'm curious about why you chose me, too, Aldrea," I said, speaking out loud for Rachel's benefit. "We all thought you'd go for Rachel or Toby."

<I don't know,> Aldrea finally admitted. <I have no memory of making the choice. The first thing I was aware of was being in your body.>

Maybe it was because she'd been able to feel my admiration for what she had done by becoming Hork-Bajir.

No, that didn't make sense. I wasn't the only one who believed her decision to defy her own people to fight the Yeerks was heroic.

I relayed her answer to Rachel. I could have shared control of my mouth, perhaps, but it would have caused problems, confusion. I didn't want to give her any more than she needed. But

neither did I want to make her hostile by treating her with suspicion. *I don't think Miss Manners covers this particular social situation,* I thought.

<Aldrea, perhaps we could both access my speech centers. If we are each careful, we may avoid problems.>

"Yes," she said.

"Yes what?" Rachel asked.

"I-she-jamrff-coo har dabdiligg . . ." Two minds, one mouth.

Rachel gave us a fish eye. "Uh-huh. And meanwhile, back at the psych ward . . ."

<Go ahead, Aldrea,> I said.

"I thought I'd been given a ridiculous receptacle at first," Aldrea admitted, speaking to Rachel almost as if I weren't there to hear. "I didn't know how I would be able to fight in this soft little body. No blades of any kind. It doesn't even have hidden poison sacs!"

"Yeah, but she has an enema bag she uses on raccoons," Rachel joked.

"But now that I know it has morphing abilities, I'm sure it will work well enough," Aldrea continued.

It. I guess "it" is the right word to use when you're talking about a body. "It" stepped in to reach the speech centers.

"So, are you ready to try this?" I asked. "I'm

concentrating on my wolf DNA right now. Can you sense it?"

<Yes,> Aldrea answered.

"To start to morph all you need to do is —" I said.

<You're forgetting that I was born an Andalite,> Aldrea answered. <We invented the morphing technology.>

Her superior tone reminded me of Ax. Every once in a while he makes it clear how primitive our human technology still is.

I could have asked her how many times she'd morphed. How many animals. I could have pointed out that my friends and I were probably the galactic morphing champions. But I didn't feel right. I felt . . . I don't know. Aldrea was a hero right out of history. And I was the girl with the raccoon enema bag.

"Well, go ahead, then," I mumbled.

I felt the tip of my nose turn wet and cold. But only for an instant. My fingernails grew thicker and longer. But a second later they returned to their usual shape.

"You're fighting me, Cassie," Aldrea said.

"Oh. Sorry. I didn't know," I answered. "Go ahead."

I felt Aldrea begin to concentrate on the wolf DNA. I started to take a deep breath, then I real-

ized that right now she should be controlling the breathing. The changes began again. The bones in my legs cracked as the joints reversed direction. The skin on my arms itched as coarse hair popped through it. Morphing has always been creepy. This time it was terrifying. Each sensation felt magnified by a hundred. I wanted to scream as I felt my intestines shift and my ribs contract.

I ordered myself to get a grip. I decided to pretend I was watching a movie. I even tried to imagine I could feel the nubby material of the theater seat behind my back and the sticky floor under my feet.

When my lips began to stretch away from my face, I tried to think of it as a cool special effect in the *Aldrea: Alien Werewolf* movie.

It helped a little. Very little.

I fell forward on my hands. No, my paws. They were paws now. A moment later, the transformation was complete.

Aldrea took off running through the forest. I could feel her exhilaration. She felt powerful and free.

I felt as if I was locked in a speeding car with no brakes and no steering wheel. I tried to hold on to the image of the movie theater I'd created, but I couldn't. Not with Aldrea racing straight toward a huge pine tree! If we hit that tree at this speed there wouldn't just be a splash of fake movie blood. There would be an explosion of very real pain.

<Aldrea, look out!> I shouted.

She swerved, missing the tree by inches.

<What were you doing? You almost bashed my — our — head in,> I cried.

<What are you talking about?> Aldrea shot back. <This morph has excellent reflexes.>

She was right. I'd probably come that close to trees dozens of times when I was in wolf morph.

Aldrea was obviously having no problems controlling the body. I just had to trust her. Except she wasn't from Earth. What if a situation came up that she couldn't recognize? Would I be able to take over the body quickly enough to deal?

I decided to try a little experiment. Without saying anything to Aldrea, I tried to wag my — our — wolf tail.

It didn't move.

I tried again, concentrating all my energy on the muscles in the tail. The tail gave a twitch. It wasn't exactly a full-out wag. But at least it moved.

<What are you doing, Cassie?> Aldrea asked. She slowed from a run to a trot, and I got a little puff of annoyance from her.

I hesitated. I didn't want to admit I'd been trying to see what kind of control I had.

Rachel loped up beside us in her own wolf morph. I couldn't help thinking that if Rachel had been in my situation she would have gotten a lot more than a pathetic little twitch out of the tail.

Rachel would not have been intimidated by Aldrea. She'd have laid down the law: Do what I tell you, or else.

Or else what, though? That was the question, wasn't it. Or else . . . what?

I wondered again why Aldrea hadn't chosen Rachel as her receptacle. But maybe the answer was all too clear: Maybe I'd been chosen because she sensed that I was the weakest.

Had she felt that I would be the easiest to control? Had Aldrea, even in her inchoate *Ixcila* form, marked me as an easy victim?

CHAPTER 10

"Okay, there's that girl, Holly Perry, you know, she transferred from Polk?" Marco said from his seat on one of the big bales of hay in my barn. "I want my Chee to ask her out for me. I tried a couple of times, but this thing happened with my voice."

"He started clucking like the chicken he is," Rachel commented.

"Holly Perry. No problem," Erek the Chee told Marco. "It's not like we have anything else to do but work on your love life. Yeah, the Chee who plays you will also hold down his regular full-time job as a restaurant manager, but hey, your love life comes first."

Marco nodded. "Good. As long as we have our priorities clear."

Aldrea was completely lost. It was comforting to feel her confusion. <The Chee are androids,> I explained. <They can throw holograms around themselves to change their appearances. While we're gone, Erek's going to get a few of them to take our places at home and school. Passing as us.>

"If we're not back before the date, my Chee should just go out with her and make sure she really has fun," Marco continued.

"Do you think that's a good idea?" Rachel asked. "Won't Holly be disappointed when she goes out with the real you?"

I felt impatience from Aldrea. The emotional wall between us was becoming more of a sieve. Her thoughts were still beyond my reach, but I could "feel" her now as a person more inside me than out.

<It's their way of blowing off steam. You know, of dealing with the anxiety of leaving for a mission,> I explained to her.

Her impatience didn't lessen. <You are all still such children,> she muttered.

<Actually, we're not much younger than you and Dak Hamee were when you fought the Yeerks.>

I got the strong feeling that she didn't appreciate the comparison.

"Any other instructions?" Erek asked.

"Ask whoever is me not to be so nice to my sisters this time," Rachel answered. "They get to expecting it."

Erek smiled. "Jake? Cassie? Anything?"

Jake shook his head. I could tell that in his thoughts at least, he'd already left Earth far behind.

"Maybe I shouldn't ask this," I said slowly. "Maybe it's bad luck or something. But if we . . . if we don't come back, would . . ." I couldn't finish the sentence. A terrible grief welled up beneath my own less intense worry.

It took me a moment to realize that most of it was coming from Aldrea. My thoughts had made her think of her own parents and her little brother. All lost to her forever.

"We could stay with your families," Erek said. "If you really wish."

"No," I said quickly. "Forget it. No. I . . . I don't think I want anyone being me permanently."

Erek nodded. "No. I've lived a long, long time. Seen a lot of death. I've never seen the point in denying death. People die. People grieve. It's better than playing games with it." He turned to go.

"Oh, Erek, one more thing," Marco called after him. "I kind of need a makeup paper on some

great figure from American history. It's kind of due day after tomorrow."

"How about Franklin Roosevelt? I was the White House butler during his administration. I was the one who came up with the phrase 'New Deal.' Of course, it was during a poker game."

CHAPTER 11

For the second time in less than one full day, we were flying to the Hork-Bajir valley.

No one was talking. Marco and Rachel weren't bothering with their usual exchange of insults. Aldrea wasn't even communicating with me in our private shared-mind communication.

Jake wasn't saying much to me, either. He couldn't talk to me, even to reassure me, without talking to Aldrea, too. I knew he was aware of potential problems there.

I felt relieved when I spotted Quafijinivon, Toby, and the other Hork-Bajir already gathered around the small Yeerk spacecraft. It was larger than a Bug fighter, but still fairly small. Instead of the cockroach-shell shape with the twin serrated Dracon cannon, it was closer to the oval shape the Andalites use, with an engine pod on either side. But the Dracon cannon were slung underneath rather than mimicking a raised tail.

I wanted to get on that ship as quickly as possible. The only way to complete this mission was to begin it. The only way to return to Earth was to leave it. The only way to regain the sole use of my body was to allow Aldrea to use it now.

I was ready. I had to be ready. That choice was made for me when Aldrea chose her receptacle.

I tucked my wings close to my body and let myself drop to the ground. I demorphed quickly.

"Anyone who doesn't have a Hork-Bajir morph, get one now," Jake instructed before the feathers had all disappeared from his face.

I stepped up to Jara Hamee and reached toward him. "May I?" I asked.

"Jara help," he answered.

I pressed my hands against his leathery chest. Aldrea fought to resist a renewed wave of grief. I couldn't figure out why for a minute, then I realized that touching Jara must remind her of how it felt to touch Dak Hamee.

It was all new to her. A loss that had occurred before I was born had happened to Aldrea just hours before. I couldn't stop thinking of it all as a story. Dak Hamee was history to me. To Aldrea he was a living, breathing person.

I acquired Jara's DNA as quickly as possible and slid my hands away. <You still really miss him, don't you?> I asked Aldrea.

<He died yesterday. And I was not with him. I did not hold his hand and tell him I loved him. Maybe in reality, but not in my memory, which is all the truth I have.>

<I'm sorry.> The words felt totally lame. But I didn't know what else to say. Aldrea said nothing more.

"It is time," Quafijinivon announced.

He took a step toward the ship, leading the way, then stopped and turned back to the expectant Hork-Bajir.

"Friend Hork-Bajir: I am deeply grateful for the gift of your DNA. I will do everything in my power to aid the new colony in banishing the Yeerks from your home planet. Believe me, or do not, but I tell you that I, the last of the Arn, will atone for the sins of my people."

Of course the Hork-Bajir didn't grasp half of this little speech. But they caught the tone.

Jara Hamee slapped his hand against his chest. "Free or dead!" he exclaimed.

"Free or dead!" Ket Halpak echoed. She slapped her hand against her own chest.

The other Hork-Bajir joined in the cry.

"Free or dead!"

Thump!

"Free or dead!"

Thump!

My eyes began to sting. I didn't know if it was my emotions or Aldrea's that caused the tears to form. In that moment our feelings were almost identical.

"Okay, let's go," Jake said.

Aldrea and I took one last look at the Hork-Bajir. We thumped our hand against our chest. "Free or dead!" we shouted.

"We" is the only way I can describe the experience. I'm really not sure if it was my voice or hers that uttered the Hork-Bajir battle cry. For that moment, the wall between us was down.

But as we made our way to the ship's door, I felt Aldrea pull away from me. I pulled away a little, too.

We were still almost strangers to each other. We both needed a little privacy. I stepped into the ship, Marco right behind me.

"Hey, all right. A hot tub," he exclaimed. "All you ladies are invited to join me." I followed his gaze to the small, drained Yeerk pool that dominated the only "room."

"It's empty," Quafijinivon reassured us. "I'll

take the helm. We will translate to Zero-space as soon as we clear the atmosphere. I must prepare for the trip to the Arn planet."

"The Hork-Bajir planet," Rachel muttered, with a significant look at me.

Quafijinivon didn't appear to hear her. He squatted uncomfortably, leaning back against a captain's chair designed for Hork-Bajir. The space beside him was without any chair, appropriate for a Taxxon.

Ax went to look over the controls. <This is a newer-generation Yeerk ship,> Ax commented. Then, his thought-speak tone elaborately casual, he said, <They've made some small innovations since they acquired the original Andalite technology from . . . well, we all know who gave the Yeerks the capacity for Z-space travel.>

"My father," Aldrea answered defiantly. "My father, Prince Seerow. Without my father, the Yeerks would never have had the opportunity to spread their evil," she continued. "Without my father, we would not all be risking our lives on this mission. That is the point the Andalite wishes to make."

<Aldrea, stop,> I begged. <No one blames you.>

She ignored me.

"All this is true," Aldrea insisted. "It is also

true that my father did what he believed was right. He believed he was helping a worthy race to advance."

<They advanced across the Hork-Bajir and now the humans.>

Aldrea whipped her — our — head toward him. "What he did is not so different from giving these humans the power to morph. And who did that, Aximili-Esgarrouth-Isthill? I know they could not have developed the technology on their own."

<You cannot compare your father to my brother,> Ax began to protest.

"Oh, but I can!" Aldrea cried triumphantly. "If your brother gave the humans the power to morph, that means he gave an inferior species technology they were incapable of developing themselves. That is all my father did."

"Wait a minute, are you comparing humans to Yeerks?" Rachel demanded. "Is that what I'm hearing?"

"Well, we're off to a good start," Marco said with a laugh. "We haven't even gotten to the first rest stop and already the kids are fighting in the backseat."

<You know, Ald —> Tobias began to say.

"Okay. Discussion over," Jake said. Tobias fell silent in mid-word. I could feel Aldrea's incredulity at being silenced by what she saw as an alien youth.

"We have to be a team here," Jake said in a voice so quiet it forced everyone to lean forward to listen. "We have to be able to count on each other. We're going deep into enemy territory. The Hork-Bajir planet is Yeerk-held. Ringed by Yeerk defenses. And we're relying on two people we don't know: Quafijinivon and Aldrea."

He shot me/Aldrea a hard look. "We'll be advised by Quafijinivon and Aldrea. And we'll always listen to Toby. But this is an Animorph mission."

"Meaning that *you* are in charge?" Aldrea demanded, almost laughing.

"That's exactly what I mean," Jake said.

I felt Aldrea's emotional reaction. A mix of resentment, condescension, and worry.

<Jake has led us through more missions, more battles than you and Dak ever fought,> I said, annoyed at her attitude.

Using my — our — mouth, Aldrea said, "I will follow Jake as though he were my prince."

Did she mean it? I couldn't tell.

I had the feeling Ax was about to say something snide. Jake raised his hand, cutting Ax off. "Thank you, Aldrea. It's an honor to have you on the team."

The moment passed. I saw Rachel smirking at me. No, at Aldrea.

<You care for this Jake person,> Aldrea said to me.

<Yeah. I do.>

<Like Dak and me.>

<Yeah. I guess so.> It was a disturbing comparison. Neither Dak nor Aldrea had survived their war.

<I wish you better luck than we had.>

<I'll open the observation panels,> Ax said. A moment later a ring of metal slid back, revealing windows in all directions.

My eyes went straight to the blue-and-white ball that was Earth. It was so far away already.

The ship picked up speed. It hurtled through space faster and faster.

Flash!

Earth disappeared.

<Translation into Zero-space,> Ax told us. <We should emerge somewhere in the galaxy of the Hork-Bajir planet. Depending on the current configuration of Zero-space.>

I looked around at our motley group. Four humans, a red-tailed hawk, an Andalite, a Hork-Bajir, an Arn with his back to us, and, invisible but still there, the hybrid thing called Aldrea.

I must have looked worried.

Marco caught my eye and laughed his sardonic laugh. "So. Yahtzee anyone?"

CHAPTER 12

ALDREA

I rolled over and realized that Dak was gone. I opened my eyes.

He was standing with his back to me. He was gazing out across the valley below. I stood up, started toward him, hesitated, then bent down to pick up the weapon I'd had within reach for every second of the last two years. I came up behind him, stepped around his curled-up tail, and put my arm around his waist.

We were at the edge of the small platform built seven hundred feet up in a crook of a Stoola tree's branches. We were at the far end of the valley, all the way down where it narrowed so much that the branches of trees across the valley reached and touched the branches from this side.

The Yeerks had searched the area thoroughly, hunting for surviving Hork-Bajir. The searching had been done by Hork-Bajir-Controllers. And yet we had escaped detection. Dak had taken the platform apart, buried it in the ground, then, when the search had passed, we defiantly rebuilt our little home.

"I love you, Dak."

He squeezed my arm against his chest. "Seerow is sleeping well now," he said.

"Yes. For the last few days, since the ships stopped arriving with all that noise."

A huge buildup had begun. The Yeerk forces, the forces we had fought, would be doubled.

"I fear for him, Aldrea."

I couldn't answer. My throat was choked. We had long since realized that we would not survive. We had accepted that. As well as anyone can accept the death of a loved one, or their own death.

But I could not accept it for Seerow, my son. Our son. Could not. And yet I could see no way out.

I looked to the little cradle of twigs where he lay.

"What will become of you, my sweet little one?"

He sat up. Too young to speak, and yet he

spoke. Not as a Hork-Bajir, but with fluency and ease.

"The Yeerks will take me, Mother."

"No."

"You will not save me, Mother."

"I . . . I couldn't."

"Where is Father?"

"What? He . . ." I reached, and Dak was no longer there. "He was just . . . what is happening?"

"Nightmare," the small, brown creature said. She had taken my son's place. "You're having a nightmare."

"Seerow!" I screamed.

The young Andalite sneered at me. <Did you imagine it was real, Aldrea-Iskillion-Falan? Did you think it could last?>

"Seerow! Dak! Come to me, come to me, let me . . . where are you?"

<Wake up! Wake up! Aldrea, wake up!>

"Seerow!"

I woke. Cassie, the human, had run to plunge our face into cold water.

I looked around, through her eyes. The lights had been darkened for sleep. The Andalite stood at rest, with a single stalk eye open, watching. Jake, the leader of the humans, had awakened.

"It's okay, Jake," Cassie said. "She just had a nightmare."

Seerow. Dead after a life as a Yeerk host. Dak. Dead, I knew not how. All of them, all our brave soldiers, all gone.

A nightmare. A dream of death from a person already dead.

CHAPTER 13

Three days had passed. Three days of having the strange, sad, secret Andalite-turned-Hork-Bajir in my head.

Sleeping with her on the hard, cold deck. Awakened shaking, sweating, wanting to tear my head open with my bare hands as I felt the awesome grief of her nightmares.

Eating with her, if you could call the concentrated nutrient pellets food. Going to the bathroom with her.

A lot more togetherness than I'd have preferred. Bad enough figuring out how to pee in a toilet designed for Hork-Bajir. Worse doing it with an audience in your own head.

We had gotten good at sharing control of speech. I controlled everything else. I had gotten used to it. I still didn't like it.

The Arn had stayed at the helm, ignoring us for the most part. I'd learned nothing more about him. Was this really some voyage of redemption for him? Aldrea doubted it. And she knew one hundred percent more about the Arn than I knew. Jake was talking with Quafijinivon when we translated out of the blank white nothingness of Zero-space into what now seemed to be the warm, welcoming black star field.

The Arn checked his sensors.

"Quafijinivon says we are now in Hork-Bajir space. We may pass the Yeerk defenses unnoticed. Or not," Jake announced. "We should get ready. We don't know what we'll be walking into. I want everyone —"

Marco held up his hand like he was asking a question.

"Yes, Marco."

"Do we have correct change for the tolls?"

Jake blinked. Then he grinned. He and Marco have been best friends forever. Marco knows how to knock Jake down a peg when Jake starts taking his fearless leader role too seriously.

Jake sat down on the floor across from me/Aldrea.

"I don't see why we couldn't have gone Z-space the whole way," Marco whined.

Ax and Aldrea both laughed. Then they realized they were both laughing at the same thing and they both stopped laughing.

"Just say it," Marco told them. "I am but a poor Earth man, unable to understand the ways of the superior Andalite beings."

"Hork-Bajir," Aldrea corrected him.

<Aldrea, why do you —> Ax began.

A flash of green streaked by.

"Shredder fire!" Aldrea yelled, and suddenly I was up and running toward the front of the ship. She had taken control of my body! It was so sudden, so effortless.

Ax reached the "bridge" first. He leaned his torso forward and looked over Quafijinivon's shoulder.

<One of ours,> Ax said. Then he clarified. <An Andalite fighter. It must be on a deep patrol. Harassing the Yeerk defenses.>

"Can we outrun him?" Jake demanded.

"They're between us and the Arn planet," Quafijinivon answered. "We're smaller. It's possible we could outmaneuver them. But it would place us well within their firing range."

Tseeeeeew!

The Andalite fired again. A miss! But the

cold, hard data from the computer made it clear exactly how close it had come.

"Fire back!" Rachel burst out. "Knock out one of his engines or something. Enough to keep him busy until we can land. They can't follow us down."

Quafijinivon's red mouth pursed thoughtfully. "Young human, that pilot is an Andalite warrior. One of the best trained fighters in the galaxy. I cannot hope to win a battle with him."

Ax and Aldrea both said roughly the same thing, which translated to human vernacular was, <You've got that right.>

<We can't fire on an Andalite,> Tobias said. He was flapping a little nervously, being tossed around as the Arn swung the ship into an evasive maneuver.

"So we let him shoot us down?" Rachel demanded. "There's one of him, eight of us. Or nine."

The Andalite fighter was coming back around in a tight, swift arc. In a few seconds his weapons would come to bear on us.

"Ax?" Jake asked.

<I cannot fire on a fellow Andalite who is merely doing his duty. Do not ask me,> Ax pleaded. <Maybe I could communicate —>

"No!" Aldrea interrupted. "If the Yeerks pick up a voice transmission, we're dead. They'll vector everything they have at us. We'll all be killed and so will the Andalites."

"Here he comes," Toby said.

I looked — and my stomach rolled over.

The Andalite fighter was on us. Seconds from firing.

This time he wouldn't miss.

CHAPTER 14

Ax leaped. He dragged the willing Arn out of the way and grabbed the controls.

<Computer, lateral thrusters, left side, full burn!> Ax cried.

WHAM!

I flew back into Toby. We both crashed to the ground. One of her blades nicked my arm and I felt a trickle of warm blood.

Everyone who'd been standing was pinned against the left side of the ship. An invisible force pushed me, forced the air out of my lungs, squeegeed my cheeks back against my ears.

Tseeeeew! Tseeeeeew!

The Andalite fighter fired.

A jolt of electricity, my hair tingled, Rachel's hair was standing straight out from her head, a blond halo. The air crackled blue. Then Rachel's hair dropped back into place.

The acceleration stopped instantly. I'd been straining forward and now, released, I tripped and fell like someone who's been tugging on a rope that snaps.

Marco landed sprawled all over me. He put his finger to his lips. "Shhh, don't tell Jake. You know how jealous he is."

<Left main engine down,> Ax reported. <And now he is angry. He is coming in slow.>

"Slow, that's good, right?" I said. I put my hand to my lip and saw blood on my fingers. I didn't even remember hitting anything.

"No, not good," Aldrea said. "He's decided we won't or can't shoot. He's coming in slow to make sure of his shot."

<Cutting lights, environmental and artificial gravity so I can give all power to the remaining engine,> Ax said.

The cabin went dark except for the glow from the control panel. And then I realized my feet were no longer glued to the floor.

"Ax, can we outmaneuver him? Yes or no?" Jake asked.

<No, Prince Jake, we cannot. But I cannot —>

Jake ignored his answer. "Aldrea?"

She knew what he was asking. I felt her ambivalence. Her hesitation.

"Yes or no!" Jake snapped.

"Yes," she said. She seized control of my body again, pushed off from the ceiling and floated weightlessly in beside Ax.

"Cripple him if you can. If not . . ." Jake said.

<Prince Jake, we cannot —> Ax pleaded.

"My decision, Ax-man," Jake said gently. "Aldrea, it's your show."

Aldrea wrapped a restraining strap over our shoulder to keep from floating away. My hands moved, taking a large, ornately designed joystick obviously constructed to accommodate Hork-Bajir fingers or Taxxon pincers. Aldrea's eyes, my eyes, were glued not to the slowly growing image of the Andalite fighter, but to the tactical weapons readout.

"Computer, go to manual firing mode," my voice said.

I watched the crosshairs on the screen swing across the field of stars and come to rest on the Andalite ship. Dead on the cockpit.

<If you were not in my friend Cassie my tail blade would be at your throat now,> Ax said in thought-speak only Aldrea and I could hear. <Do not miss.>

Aldrea moved my fingers again, ever so slightly,

gently, caressing the targeting crosshairs till they centered on the Andalite's right-side engine pod.

Had she retargeted because of Ax's threat? Or had she always intended to aim for the engine? In either case, a miss would likely mean a direct hit on the Andalite ship itself.

HMMMMMMMM . . .

TSEEEEEEW!

A single shot. The red Dracon beam punched through the blackness. Stabbed at the Andalite ship. Then a pale, orange explosion. The engine pod blew apart. The Andalite ship spun wildly, falling away from us.

"Yes!" Rachel cried as she drifted in midair, almost upside down. "You clipped an engine!"

<Targets approaching!> Ax yelled. <Multiple . . . I count four!> He swung his stalk eyes backward to look at Jake. <Yeerk Bug fighters. They are coming to finish him off.>

"Can he fly?" Jake asked.

<Yes. He is regaining control. But he is as slow as we are, now. He will never outrun them.>

"They won't attack us," Marco remarked. "They see we fired on the Andalite. We're a bona fide Yeerk craft."

<How lucky for us,> Ax said acidly. <That warrior has bought us our passage.>

"We just keep flying, we're home free," Marco pointed out.

Quafijinivon said, "Yes, yes! Keep flying."

One by one we looked at Jake. "Nah, I don't think so," he said.

Marco smiled. "I had a premonition you'd say that."

"Ax? Aldrea? Four of them. If we fire on the Yeerks, will the Andalite figure it out? Will he join in?"

<Yes!> Ax said. <He is already wondering why we do not finish him off.>

"Okay," Jake said. "Wait. Wait till you can't possibly miss your first shot. Then, boom! Boom! Boom! Boom! Four shots. Hit or miss it'll confuse the Yeerks, scare the slime off them."

Four Bug fighters loomed up from the brilliant crescent of the planet below, racing around their orbit toward us, engines blazing.

The Andalite ship seemed to be drifting now, helpless.

"Is he really —" Marco asked.

"No," Aldrea said. "He's hurt but not that badly. He's playing dead to draw the Yeerks in. He'll take one last shot. That's his plan. One shot and then die."

It was Tobias, the instinctual flier who saw the possibilities. <Hey, we drift left, get behind the Andalite, the Yeerks may hesitate to shoot, thinking we're friendly and they might hit us. They'll split left and right to get a safe angle of attack.

At that speed, that angle, you hit the left-side leader and —>

"And the debris will shred the following ship!" Aldrea said enthusiastically.

Ax hit lateral positioning thrusters for just a second, then we drifted, seemingly without power.

The Yeerks saw us in their line of fire, split left and right, just as Tobias had . . .

TSEEEEEEW! TSEEEEEW!

We fired.

BOOOM!

The left-side lead Bug fighter blew apart.

Tseeeeew!

The Andalite fired. The right-side leader exploded.

The left-side leader plowed into his partner's debris. An engine erupted. Ripped loose, sliced open the entire back end of the Bug fighter, which spun, then BOOOM!

Three Bug fighters down in less than ten seconds.

The Andalite fired his one good engine and went after the remaining Yeerk. But not before giving a slight roll to his ship. A sort of wave.

<Good hunting, brother,> Ax said.

Everyone started cheering.

"Good shooting, Ax and Cassie!" Rachel crowed.

"Yes, good work," Jake said much more quietly. "We may have just alerted the Yeerks, made things harder. So take five seconds to celebrate, then get ready to land. Be ready for battle morphs if needed."

<Cassie, I believe I like your boyfriend,> Aldrea said.

CHAPTER 15

ALDREA

Down. Down through the clouds, through the atmosphere that made the hull scream. Down to my home. The planet I had never left, and yet now returned to.

"The Yeerk automated defenses appear to have accepted our codes," Quafijinivon said.

"That would be a good thing?" Rachel asked.

"If they did not accept our identification they would have targeted us with ground-based Dracon cannon. We have another threshold to cross when we enter the valley proper."

I hadn't seen it from space since I first arrived with my family. My father, in disgrace, but acting as though he didn't know that this was a dead-end, irrelevant assignment for an Andalite whose

name had become a derisive joke, a synonym for "fool."

With my mother, just happy to have new, unclassified species to study. With my brother, who felt our humiliation so much more deeply than me.

All dead, of course. I'd seen them die in the blistering Dracon beam attack from low-flying Yeerk Bug fighters.

It was not a beautiful planet, at least not to Andalite sensibilities. An Andalite sought instinctively for the vast expanses of open grass, the delicate pastel trees, the meandering rivers and streams.

But the Hork-Bajir planet was scarred by the impact of the asteroid or moonlet that had erased its former character. The surface was barren, cracked, and fissured. The cracks were miles wide and miles deep, with shockingly steep sides. Life on the planet existed now only in those valleys.

There the giant trees soared. There the Hork-Bajir had once lived in peaceful ignorance, praising Mother Sky and Father Deep, harvesting the bark, avoiding the monsters that guarded the depths of the valleys.

We skimmed the barrens and then, suddenly, dropped into the valley. Dak's valley. My valley.

I looked and was suddenly glad that Cassie

had control of my body. If she didn't, I may not have been able to remain standing.

The trees! The trees! So many gone. The valley walls had been scarred, stripped. The Yeerks had cut deep gashes into the valleys to make level spaces.

"You must remember that it has been years since you last saw your home," Quafijinivon told me.

But it wasn't the years that had ravaged the trees. It was the Yeerks. More than half of them, gone. Pieces of most of the others had been blasted away.

<I should have known . . . I should have expected . . .> I said to Cassie.

Even before I . . . before I died, some of the trees had been destroyed. But now it was as if the planet had been massacred. For the trees were the planet.

"We appear to have been accepted and registered by the inner-defense grid," Quafijinivon said, breathing a sigh. "This is fortunate. We pass within a hundred yards of Dracon cannon in the valley walls."

"I can't believe we haven't reached the ground yet," Jake said. "How tall are these trees?"

I knew he expected me to answer. But I couldn't.

"The largest are two thousand feet tall," Quafijinivon answered. "The trunks a hundred feet in diameter. They are a masterpiece of Arn bio-engineering."

<Aldrea, are you all right?> Cassie asked softly.

<Turn away,> I begged. I hated the weakness in my voice, but I couldn't bear to look anymore. <Turn our eyes away.>

She did. But then, she looked again. And I looked, too. Because even now, scarred and blasted, raped and despoiled, it was my home.

"Two minutes," Quafijinivon said. "We will land just above the vapor barrier, within the former range of the monsters we created to restrain Hork-Bajir curiosity."

I felt the tension rise in Cassie. This was all alien to her, of course. A strange world.

For me it was familiar, and yet not. I had, in my mind, never left. The years had not passed. The change seemed sudden, massive, shocking. The destruction of decades in the blink of an eye.

But it was Toby who interested me. This was her ancestral home. A place she had never seen, but that must, in some way, be part of the substructure of her Hork-Bajir mind.

She was staring out of the window with curiosity, even fascination. But Hork-Bajir faces show little emotion. What she felt, if anything, remained a mystery. We would be landing, soon, and I didn't even know my own mind. I did not trust the Arn. I did not like the Andalite, but trusted him to be what he was.

I didn't know the humans, not even the one whose brain I shared. The one named Jake had performed well.

But I did not know what was ahead. I knew only one thing: Whether the Arn was true to his word or plotting some betrayal, it didn't matter. I had seen what the future held for my adopted world. And all my doubt, my cynicism born of exhaustion, was wiped away.

I, who had never left, was back. And I would make the Yeerks pay. No matter the cost.

I sensed the human, Cassie, reading my emotions, listening for clues. I was being careless. I closed my mind to her and sealed off my emotions.

CHAPTER 16

I felt the ship gently touch down. I felt the wall inside me go up.

I couldn't blame Aldrea. If the situation were reversed, I don't think I'd want to witness all the ways Earth had been violated by war and then have some second person reading my first thoughts.

"We have made it," Quafijinivon said with some satisfaction. "We are home. I will open the hatch and —"

"Hold up," Jake said. "What's out there? Should we morph to Hork-Bajir?"

Quafijinivon shook his head. "We're just above the Arn valley, in the no-man's-land. The

Yeerks don't come here now that all the monsters are dead. And, of course, they think all the Arn are dead as well." He gave a sad, dusty-sounding laugh.

He led the way to the ship's exit bay. I couldn't help noticing that his legs were slightly unsteady.

When I stepped onto the ramp, I was struck by how bright it was outside. That's really all I noticed at first — the intensity of the light and the way the sky almost seemed to glow.

"I must start my work soon, or risk a degradation of the DNA I harvested," Quafijinivon said. "My lab is not far. Follow me."

He led the way across a gently angled space of scrub bushes and weeds that ended abruptly in a jaw-dropping cliff that went straight down seemingly forever.

"You may not be aware of this, but not all of us have wings," Rachel pointed out. "At least not at the moment."

"There are steps," Quafijinivon assured us without turning around.

I gingerly approached the drop-off and peered down. Straight down almost nothing could be seen. But across the narrow chasm I could see that the far side was carved with doorways, windows, archways, and walkways. They were cut di-

rectly into the stone. Sections had been blasted away by Dracon beams, perhaps long ago, but the Arn village was still beautiful.

Jake said, "Tobias?"

Tobias flapped his wings, took to the air, and soared out over the valley. He floated for several minutes, using his laser-focus hawk's eyes to look down and around. Then he swooped back.

<I don't see anything alive down there,> he reported. <Pity. It's a stunning place. It must have been something when it was all inhabited.>

"Yeah. It looks like those Anasazi cliff dwellings in New Mexico or wherever," Marco said.

Rachel gave him a look. "Since when do you even know the word 'Anasazi'?"

"I've told you guys before, every now and then I stay awake in class. Just for a change."

Quafijinivon led us down a narrow stone staircase. There was no guardrail.

<It's times like these I appreciate my wings,> Tobias said. <I'd be real careful. You fall off and you'll have a long time to think about it on the way down.>

Jake, Rachel, Tobias, Ax, Marco, and Toby started down the side of the cliff after Quafijinivon. I fell in at the end of their single-file line. I wasn't happy about it. I'm not crazy about walking on cliffs. But it's not like I had a choice.

I locked my eyes on my feet, watching them

as they moved from step to step. If Aldrea was feeling any fear, or any contempt of my fear, she wasn't letting me know about it. She'd sealed up the wall between us and every brick was still in place.

"What's that red and yellow gunk at the bottom?" Marco called. "It looks like it's moving."

"Oh, thank you, Marco," I muttered. "Right now I really need to be thinking about what's way, way, way down there."

"It is the core of the planet," Quafijinivon answered.

"The core," Rachel repeated. "You're talking core as in center?"

"Yes, of course," he answered. His tone made it clear that he thought she was a little on the slow side.

"So, it's like a volcano down there, with lava and everything," Marco said. "How hot is that lava? You know, in case we fell in?"

"You're not helping," I told him, without raising my eyes from my feet. "Really not."

<You do not have to worry about the lava, Cassie,> Ax comforted me.

"Thanks, Ax," I answered.

<If you fell, I believe you would be incinerated before you hit the actual magma,> he continued.

Sometimes I think hanging around Marco so

much has given Ax a totally twisted sense of humor. Very un-Andalite.

Quafijinivon turned at one of the arches. One by one, we followed him into a long, narrow room, almost a cave.

For the first time since we started down the side of the cliff, I raised my eyes from my feet. I watched as Quafijinivon pressed a small blue pad set in one wall.

An instant later the whole wall slid open. A row of long, clear cylinders and an elaborate computer console filled most of the room.

"It took me years to piece together all the equipment I needed for a new lab," Quafijinivon said. "The Yeerk raids destroyed almost everything."

"I've never heard of Yeerks using Arn hosts," Toby said. "I understood the Arn spared themselves that by altering their own physiology."

"True, Seer," the Arn said. "The Yeerks did not kill us in pursuit of hosts. It was a game. A sport. My people were exterminated, our culture destroyed, because the Yeerks enjoyed using us for target practice."

The Arn's voice held only an echo of a bitterness that must go very deep.

Then the strange creature shuffled away. "I have work to do."

CHAPTER 17

ALDREA

Home. Planet of the Hork-Bajir. My planet.

I was desperate to escape from the soft, slow human body and feel my true form again. I wanted to be Hork-Bajir.

"Okay, we aren't here to sightsee," Jake said. "We're here to retrieve the weapons Aldrea and Dak hid. We find them, we tell Quafijinivon where to pick them up, and he flies us all home."

"Toby is already home," I said.

Toby looked up sharply. The idea surprised her.

"This is your home world, Toby," I said.

<Toby wants to stay that will be her call,> the *nothlit* hawk said. <The rest of us, me, Ax, Jake,

Rachel, Marco, and Cassie? We're all going home.>

The emphasis on "all" would have been impossible to miss. The creature named Tobias was warning me.

And what, I wondered, *would you be able to do if I decide that Cassie stays here?* But I said nothing. The humans and the obnoxious Andalite were already suspicious of me. Paranoid. Aximili was more concerned about me than about the Yeerks.

I had no allies in this group. With the possible exception of Toby. She was, after all, my great-granddaughter.

<Aldrea, he's waiting for an answer.>

<What?>

<Jake asked you a question.>

"I'm sorry, I didn't hear you," I said aloud.

"Are you ready? You're our guide. Take us to the weapons. Let's get this moving."

"Yes, I'm ready," I said. I tried to cover the uncertainty I felt, tried to hide it from Cassie.

I did not know the location of the weapons. I remembered Dak and I and the others, the few who still gathered with us, taking the ship. But I must have hidden them after recording my *Ixcila.*

<You don't know where they are!> Cassie accused.

<Nonsense!>

<Oh, my God! You don't! I can feel it. I can tell you're lying.>

<I know where I planned to put them. I know where they must be.>

<We have to tell Jake.>

<No!>

She opened her mouth. "J — . . . unh . . . Ja . . ."

<Let me talk!>

I released my hold, shocked at my own behavior. I hadn't meant to stop her, hadn't meant to battle for control. A mistake; I'd had no time to think it through.

Everyone was staring at me. All but the Arn who was busy elsewhere.

<Don't ever do that again, Aldrea,> Cassie said.

<I —>

<Don't ever fight me for control again.> Then she opened our — her — mouth and said, "She doesn't know where the weapons are. Not for sure. She has an idea."

Andalite facial expressions are subtle. But I had been born an Andalite. I saw the triumph in Aximili's eyes. The sense that he had judged me correctly.

Human facial expressions were still strange to me. Jake's face showed nothing. It seemed to be deliberately void of expression.

"That's something we should have thought about before we took off," he said mildly.

<May I use your mouth to speak?> I asked Cassie.

<Go ahead.>

"I am confident I can find the weapons. I know where I would have hidden them. Where I intended to hide them."

"That's great," Marco snapped, "but there's a big difference between getting yourself killed for a 'definitely' as opposed to a 'possibly.'"

"No one will be in danger. I know the place. I know the trees."

Jake said, "No choice now. We're here. But, you, Aldrea, are no longer to be trusted. You're mad at the Andalites, mad at the Arn, and you don't treat humans as allies. I understand your anger. You're in a very strange reality right now. But we get in and out alive, that's what we do. So if you get in the way, make me doubt you again, we will put you down."

I bridled at the insult and the threat. "This is my world, human. My battle. Follow me, do as I say, and you will soon be able to scurry back to Earth."

Rachel said, "And you'll be back in Quafijinivon's bottle."

"That's right," I said.

Jake took a deep breath and then said, "We

want to avoid Earth morphs if we can. No point announcing 'The Animorphs are here.' We'll travel as Hork-Bajir. All but Tobias. I want you in the air, man. But stay out of view if possible."

<On my way,> the *nothlit* said. He spread his wings, flew along the ground for a while, then flapped up and away into the mist.

"Okay. Now we morph."

CHAPTER 18

ALDREA

<I assume you will control the morph,> I said to Cassie.

<Yes, I will,> she said.

I waited as she focused her mind on the Hork-Bajir DNA within her.

The changes began with surprising swiftness. Cassie was an experienced morpher, that much was clear. But as I watched the smooth, elegant transitions, I realized she was more than experienced. She was talented.

Her five-foot-tall frame expanded upward, growing like a sapling, shooting up by a full two feet. The muscles layered over her own weaker human musculature. The bones became dense.

The internal organs shifted with a liquid sound, some disappearing altogether, others appearing, forming, finding a place, making connections, beginning to secrete and digest and filter.

Her heel bone grew a spur, the Hork-Bajir back toe. Her own five human toes melted together, then split and grew into three long claws.

The tail grew as an extension of her spine, adding link upon link, bone growing from bone, wrapping itself in flesh and blood vessels and skin.

Her flat mouth pushed outward, lips stretching into a hideous grimace then softening into the familiar Hork-Bajir smile.

Then she did something I did not know could be done: She controlled the appearance of the blades so that they appeared, one by one, rippling up one arm, down the other, down a leg, up the next.

The horns grew the same way, one, two, three. She was showing off. Trying to impress me. And I was impressed.

<You have a talent for morphing,> I said.

<Thanks.>

I saw the subtle evolution from human to Hork-Bajir eyes. Colors shifted as the spectrum of visible light moved toward the ultraviolet, losing color toward the infrared end of the spectrum.

I saw the planet of the Hork-Bajir as a Hork-Bajir. I was truly home. Myself once more. Not a female, a male, but that was irrelevant.

I was Hork-Bajir!

All the others were completing their morphs. I was back with my adopted people. Or at least the illusion of my own people. And in my life as it was, at this moment, nothing could be free of illusion.

<Lead the way,> Jake said, obviously preferring to use thought-speak rather than struggle with the difficult Hork-Bajir diction.

<Cassie, I want . . . it would be best if I controlled this body, for now.>

<Okay. Do it.>

I pointed upward, out of the valley. "To the trees!"

We ran up the narrow stairs. Hork-Bajir did not fear heights. Up the stairs, across the barrens, feeling the slope grow ever more steep. Up through the mist. And then, still at a run, my head rose through the mist and saw the first tree.

Huge! It was a curved wall, a monstrous Stoola tree. My hearts leaped. I ran straight for it. Cassie ran. The Hork-Bajir ran. Andalite, human, Hork-Bajir all become one in the excitement of running, running, then leaping up, digging blades into the soft bark.

I was climbing. The experience that was so strange for an Andalite had been so strange for me for so long and was now so familiar.

To my surprise the human Cassie was both afraid of the growing height and, at a deeper level, strangely comfortable racing up toward the lowest branches a hundred feet or more up the trunk.

Of course. I should have realized: the arms that hinge through three hundred and sixty degrees, the strong hands with opposable thumbs, the feet with vestigial fingers.

<You humans are a brachiating species?> I asked.

<Of course. Our ancestors, the species that came before humans evolved, lived in the trees.>

<I felt that you were more at peace than an Andalite would have been.>

<Yeah, as long as we don't fall.>

<Hork-Bajir do not fall from the trees.>

Up and up, toes and blades biting the bark, racing straight toward "Father Sky."

<These are some seriously big trees,> Marco said. <This one tree could be lawn furniture for the entire country.>

<Why are we climbing?> Rachel asked. <I mean, we want to go somewhere, right? Not just straight up?>

<This is the way to travel here,> I reassured them. <Go up to go left or right.>

<I've been telling them that for a long time,> Tobias remarked. <Altitude is everything.>

<How's it look, Tobias?> Jake asked.

<I don't see any Hork-Bajir, or anything else except some small, fuzzy, monkey-looking things.>

<Chadoo,> I said.

<Whatever. Aside from that I just see some really, really large trees. I mean, these trees are up in my face. I don't mind flying through branches for a while, but I'm used to the air above two hundred feet being wide-open.>

We reached a long branch that ran almost level toward the south. Toward the valley's end where Dak and I lived. Had lived. Had given birth to Seerow.

If I had hidden weapons, it would be there.

And it was my home. A week ago, to my mind, it had been home.

I had to see it.

CHAPTER 19

Run!

We raced along the branch. Ran at full speed on a curved, uneven, knotted branch.

Ran like giant squirrels, sure-footed, and yet, within a few inches of falling and falling and . . .

The end of the branch!

<Aldrea, the branch is — AAAAAHHHH!>

Leap! Fly! Falling, arms outstretched, falling, wind whipping by, a flash of Tobias, leaves the size of circus tents.

She stuck out a hand. Grabbed a thin branch, I could close my hand around it, too small to hold us, oh God, we were going to die.

Falling, the branch bending down and down

and down and then, slower, slower, uh-oh, uh-oh, we were going back up! Spring action now whipped us up at dizzying, insane speeds, a giant rubber band, a slingshot, and at the top of the arc, she released.

<Aaaahhhhhh!>

We flew, somersaulted, and fell, down, down, THUNK!

My Hork-Bajir feet bit into a new branch, a new tree.

<Okay, that was nuts!> I yelled. <Let's do it again!>

The others were following, move for move, more or less.

We took off again, more businesslike now, but still swinging wildly from branch to branch, tree to tree in a trapeze act like no one on Earth had ever seen.

Aldrea stopped finally and rested. She watched the others catch up. More specifically, she watched Toby. The young Hork-Bajir seer was blazing through the trees, smiling, laughing.

<She's all I have left,> Aldrea said.

<You must have relatives,> I said. <Andalite relatives.>

<She is all I have,> Aldrea insisted. <And I don't even have her. I have oblivion.>

I felt a chill. Aldrea was right. This person,

this Andalite or Hork-Bajir, whatever she was who shared space in my brain, had nothing. She was not alive. Not truly alive.

Unless . . .

Unless she refused to return to oblivion.

It occurred to me then, for the first time, that Aldrea could live, through me, if I permitted it.

No! No, this wasn't up to me. Was it?

She was alive, now. Alive in a way. She spoke and thought and felt and experienced and even learned. She was alive, but only by my grace.

Oh, my God. Was it my decision to make? Would I have to tell her when the time had come to return to nothingness?

Was I going to be the one to kill Aldrea-Iskillion-Falan?

The realization took my breath away. Aldrea felt my emotions.

<What is the matter?> she asked.

I couldn't answer. What could I say? If I'd realized before I accepted the *Ixcila* I'd never have agreed to go along. It was impossible. It was immoral. Aldrea was alive, and if she died again, if she ceased to exist, it would come from my own selfishness.

There it was, I thought, the fatal weakness that had drawn Aldrea's *Ixcila* to me. At some subrational, instinctive level, Aldrea's spirit had

sensed the weakness in me. She had known that I could not, would not, demand her death.

Tobias came swooping past. <Aldrea, how much further in this direction?> he asked.

<Another quarter mile, no more,> she said. <There is a place where the valley grows so narrow that the trees reach across it and touch each other.>

<Not anymore there isn't,> Tobias said. Then, to Jake, he said, <Trouble ahead, fearless leader.>

<What's up?>

<You'll see for yourself in a few minutes,> Tobias said grimly. <Just keep your heads down.>

CHAPTER 20

ALDREA

Hearts in my throat I raced through the trees. All familiar, a path I had traveled a hundred times, a thousand, with Dak beside me, with Seerow hanging onto my belly as we moved.

Home. It was just ahead. Home.

And somehow, somehow, he would be there, Dak, strong, smiling, holding his arms open for me.

My son, my little one, my Seerow, he would be there in his nest, waiting, smiling happily to see his mother.

Impossible. I knew. I was not insane. I knew. And yet, the hope . . . irrational hope. An emotion not touched by all that I thought I knew.

Home!

I swung faster and faster, leaving the others behind, with only the hawk for company, now.

I stopped. A clearing where there couldn't be a clearing. An open space between the branches ahead. Sky rather than leaves.

No. It couldn't be. I would die rather than see it. No.

I crept forward and now the others caught up. They stayed back, cautious, knowing something terrible had happened.

At last I did not need to go closer. I saw. A hundred trees, gone. The earth was scarred, bare. A huge, open space, naked beneath the sun.

The Yeerks had destroyed most of the valley's end. It had been dammed up. A muddy gray sludge filled a crudely constructed lake. Tree trunks formed the sides. Bisected branches formed the piers that extended out into the lake.

Only it was not a lake.

My home, my valley's end where the branches reached across the chasm to touch, was a Yeerk pool.

The others caught up to me. We all stood amid the high branches and gazed down at the devastation. The humans did not understand, of course, not really. This was my home. Not from decades ago, but from just the other day. Just the other day I left my husband and my son there. Just the other day they were alive.

<I'm sorry, Aldrea,> Cassie said.

It was true. I was dead. I saw, I heard, I touched and felt, and yet, I was dead.

This life was no life at all. This life was an illusion created by the Arn. My life was Dak. My life was Seerow. Everyone who had made up my life with theirs was gone.

I looked for any last clue to what had been. These had been trees I knew. Trees that had personalities, at least to me. They didn't have the near-sentience of some Andalite tree species, but they were individuals nevertheless.

Stoola, Nawin, Siff trees, all gone, most burned away by Dracon blasts. Those that remained had been used to form the dam. Four of them laid lengthwise, stacked, then buttressed by saplings.

Behind the dam a billion gallons of the sludge Yeerks love. I knew Yeerk pools. I had spent my youth on the Yeerk home world with my parents. This had to be one of the largest Yeerk pools in existence. It might be home to ten thousand Yeerks, even more.

Then I spotted something I knew. Barely visible from this range. A minuscule patch where the

bark had been cut away. Nothing unusual: where there are Hork-Bajir, there is scarred bark.

<Friend hawk,> I called. <I understand your sight is very powerful.>

<Better than human,> Tobias answered. <Better than Andalite or Hork-Bajir, too.>

I told him where to look. And he described what I'd known he would see: The wood where the bark had been scraped away was cut with symbolic branches entwined. A bit of Hork-Bajir graffiti. A love letter.

<The Hork-Bajir symbol for undying love,> Toby told the others. <It sounds as if it contains the Andalite letters "A" and "D," as well.>

<The weapons will be there,> I said firmly. <Inside that tree. It has a hollow base. Dak and our fellow fighters used it as a hideout. There is a chamber inside, all smooth wood, silent and dark. The chamber is forty feet, almost round. Large enough to conceal a small transport ship. We cut a wide entry, disguised, grown over with new bark after each use.>

<You said you were not sure where the weapons are,> the Andalite said.

<I said I knew where we had most likely hidden them. That is the place.>

<It is part of the dam. It will be heavily guarded. Seven of us? It would be suicide, and for what? To learn that you made a mistake?>

<We mess with that tree,> Marco said, <the whole dam may come crashing down.>

<That's what she wants,> Rachel said. <Revenge.>

I said nothing.

<The entry you talked about, can you get it to open again?> Jake asked.

<Yes. It will still work. It was precisely constructed. And the water pressure will have kept it shut.>

<Water pressure?>

<Yes. The opening is on the far side of the tree. It is beneath the surface of the Yeerk pool.>

CHAPTER 21

It was not an easy plan to work out. We needed to get into the Yeerk pool itself. We needed to be able to function underwater. Aldrea needed to be in Hork-Bajir morph in order to open the tree.

Then, if she opened it, we needed to be able to get inside, enter the ship, and figure out how to fly it out of the middle of a log a hundred feet in diameter.

The plan we hatched was pure insanity. I knew this, not because Marco pronounced it insane, he thinks everything is insane. But I knew we were in trouble when Aldrea said it was insane.

"You have a better plan?" Rachel demanded. "Because we're all ears, here."

"What you are proposing is suicide!" Aldrea argued, speaking through me.

Marco laughed. "You've got my vote."

"We need a whale," Jake said. He looked at me, at Rachel.

"I'll do it," Rachel said. "Hey, it'll be —"

"No," I interrupted. "A sperm whale has a very narrow mouth. And I'm better at controlling a morph. Faster."

Rachel argued. Jake hung his head. He'd known it had to be me. I snuck my hand into his and he squeezed it briefly.

"This is not how morphing powers are used," Aldrea said. "Let's take our time, raid the Yeerks, take weapons, perhaps capture some Hork-Bajir and starve the Yeerks out of them, then, when we have an army —"

<You and Dak Hamee, all over again?> Ax said.

"I want this attack to succeed!" Aldrea shouted. "I don't want a wasted, futile effort. You humans are just children! What do you know about fighting the Yeerks?"

"They know quite a bit, Great-grandmother," Toby said.

Jake held up his hand, cutting off debate. "The Chee can't cover for us forever. We need to

get this done and get out of here. Aldrea, yes, it's crazy. But we've been doing 'crazy' since Ax's brother showed up."

There was a vote. Aldrea pleaded with me to vote against.

<I trust Jake,> I said. <If he thinks we can do it, we can do it.>

That's what I told her. What I felt was a whole different story.

<Cassie, don't be stupid,> Aldrea urged. <It is you who will die. The others will survive, but you will be the target.>

<I know.>

<If your timing is off by a few seconds . . . too much speed . . . too much mass too early . . . Cassie, you won't just kill yourself, I am in here, too! If you are killed . . . I won't have the option of returning to a bottle and awaiting some new chance at life.>

<I know that,> I said.

She was still arguing as I morphed to osprey. Still arguing as the others all morphed to flea or fly, all as small as they could get. Only Toby would not be coming along.

Once I was completely osprey, I picked the insects up, one by one. They crouched inside my beak. Not roomy or pleasant maybe, but safe enough.

I took to the air, released my grip on a high branch and floated out over the valley, out into the Hork-Bajir night. The narrow valley funneled heat upward, an almost continuous thermal that made flying easy. I turned in a spiral, flapped, rested, flapped again, higher and higher.

I flew up till I could see the barren lands beyond the chasm. There the thermal failed, dissipated by horizontal winds. I was as high as I could go.

<That's it, boys, girls, and etcetera,> I said. <I can see the Yeerk pool. The dam is brightly lit. There's a Bug fighter more or less hovering at the far end. Hork-Bajir are patrolling the dam, walking along the top. Both banks of the pool. They have guards everywhere. So. You guys need anything before I start?>

I was trying hard to sound nonchalant. I was scared to death. I was so far up, but not far enough.

<I could use a soda,> Marco said.

<We're not the problem, Cassie,> Jake said. <Just don't open your mouth and we'll be okay. We'll start demorphing as soon as there's room.>

<Okay.>

I took a deep breath. I picked my aiming point: near the dam, but not too near. I didn't

want to hit wood. I didn't want to hit as a full-fledged whale, either. A whale at that speed would be crushed by the impact.

Speed. It was all a question of speed.

I began to demorph.

CHAPTER 22

<It can't be done!> Aldrea warned.

<Yes, it can,> I said. <I can do it. Now please, shut up. I need to focus.>

I began to demorph. My talons became pudgy and grew into toes. My feathers melted together like wax under a blowtorch.

My face flattened, my beak softened into lips. My sensitive human tongue could feel the five insects inside my mouth.

Don't open your mouth, I reminded myself. But that was only my secondary worry. That part was easy.

The hard part was keeping my wings.

I fell. Down and down through the night. Down and down toward the bright Yeerk pool be-

low. Down toward the still-oblivious sentries who could burn me out of the air.

I fell, more and more human. But my wings, my osprey wings, I kept.

Morphing is never logical or rational. Things don't happen in a neat, predictable sequence. No one can ever be sure how it will happen. But I could, with some part of my mind I couldn't even feel, some part of my brain with which I could not even communicate, shape the way the morphing happened.

Ax says I have a talent. A gift. It wasn't my doing, and I don't know where it came from or why I have it. But, as I fell and demorphed and fell, my human body, my short, pudgy human body had wings that grew and grew and spread wider than osprey wings can spread.

I couldn't flap them or even turn the edges or control a single feather, but I could hold them stiff, and as I fell, I fell . . . slowly.

<You're doing it!> Aldrea cried. <Impossible!>

I fell slowly, reusing the accelerating pull of gravity. And then, only a hundred feet above the Yeerk pool, I began to morph to whale.

My feet twined together, like fast-acting ivy, or spaghetti twirled on a fork. They melted, and fused and my flesh grew thicker, fatter.

And still, I kept the wings.

Now I was within visual range of the Hork-Bajir guards. Now they could shoot at me, any moment, if only they looked up. One head raised to look at the stars and I would be —

Tseeeeeew!

A red beam appeared five feet from my face, then disappeared.

<Let go! Fall!> Aldrea cried.

<No! It's too early!>

<Jake, they're shooting!> I reported.

<Are we close enough?>

<I don't know!> I cried. <No. No, we're not.>

<Your call, Cassie. I trust you.>

Tseeeeew!

A second shot, this one behind me. More and more Hork-Bajir were looking up, goblin heads tilted back to see me.

They would not see a human. That was vital. We could not be here, certainly could not be humans. Humans on the Hork-Bajir home world? It would cause a galaxy-wide alert and bring more pressure than ever on Visser Three to find us, at all costs.

When the Hork-Bajir looked up they saw a melting, shifting thing with wide white wings and a whale's tail.

<Let go, I tell you!>

<Not yet,> I grated.

Tseeeeeew! Tseeeeeeew!

<Aaaarrrgghh!> A hole the size of a quarter appeared in my tail fin, smoking.

Tseeeeeew! Tseeeeew! Tseeeeew!

Red beams everywhere, left, right, some so near I smelled the air burning.

<I am taking over,> Aldrea cried. I felt her will surge, a tidal wave inside my mind.

<NO!>

She was trying to fold my wings, trying to drop, reaching to take over my mind.

Tseeeeeew! Tseeeeeew!

A shot burned a seven-inch slice into my side. The pain was staggering.

My wings were . . . closing . . . losing the morph . . .

NO! This was my body, this was me!

I shoved against the tidal wave of Aldrea's will, weak hands holding back a cataclysm.

But my wings stayed firm. I fell, faster, but not too fast. Aldrea fought me, I fought back, but I still owned this body, this morph. We fell, the strange, sad Andalite turned Hork-Bajir, the dead creature with a will of iron, and me. And all the while I morphed. Morphed till my osprey wings grew heavy with flesh that was as much whale as human.

The ground fire was a wall of flame.

At last, close enough. I demorphed my wings and plunged.

CHAPTER 23

ALDREA

I had lost.

We fell, fell toward certain death, plunged tail first into the Yeerk pool, and still, all I could think was that I had lost.

Lost to a human child. I'd assumed the only question was one of self-restraint. I'd believed I could seize this body if ever I chose. But the little human female had held me at bay even as she performed an act of morphing that would have made her a hero among the Andalites.

No time to think about that. No time to think about how she could have . . . no, there was a battle to fight.

We plunged deep in the Yeerk pool and now Cassie was growing with a shocking speed, growing so huge, so fast that the body was creating little whirlpools.

<Now I need you,> Cassie said.

I almost laughed. It was outrageous. Now she needed me?

<I am here,> I said. What else could I say?

<Use my eyes. Use my echolocation. Take us to the log and the opening.>

We swam, almost blinded by sudden, seething groups of Yeerks in their natural state. But the firing was done. The Hork-Bajir-Controllers could not fire on the pool. As the human Marco had predicted. Once in the pool we were safe. Until the Yeerks could evacuate their brothers, call them to the far end of the pool.

Then they would heat the water to steam with their Dracon beams and boil us alive.

Minutes. No more. Maybe less.

<I can't see,> I said.

<I'll fire echolocation clicks,> Cassie said. <You'll see a sort of sketchy picture. Relax into it. Let it happen to you, don't strain for it.>

She fired a series of rapid sonic hiccups. I read the picture. The sketch, really, as she had said.

<Left. A hundred yards. I think. I don't know.>

We were already moving, huge tail whipping the water, scattering lingering Yeerks.

In my vast mouth, the whale's mouth, Cassie's, I felt the others demorphing, growing.

<Need some air soon,> Jake said.

Cassie kicked, changed the angle of her fins, and skimmed the surface. <Whales don't breathe through their mouths,> she explained. <I'll need to travel on the surface, keep my mouth open.>

As soon as we surfaced, the firing began.

Tseeeeew! Tseeeeew!

Misses that caused eruptions of steam. And hits that caused agony.

<Diving!> Cassie warned. <Everyone breathe deep!>

And down we plunged, turned, and stopped. <Jake. We're there.>

<We're ready.>

Pah-loosh! Pah-loosh!

<I heard something,> Cassie said.

<Taxxons. They're sending Taxxons in after us.>

<Rachel and Jake will take care of them. Demorphing, now! Jake! Three . . . two . . .>

Cassie was confident that her two friends could stop a small army of Taxxons.

We raced toward the solid wooden wall ahead. We surged, dived, then suddenly rocketed up to the surface.

Into the air! Mouth wide-open. Amazing that this monstrous beast could almost fly!

<One!> Cassie cried. <Go! Go!>

Aximili and Tobias leaped. One real Andalite,

one morphed Andalite. Marco bounded, in Hork-Bajir morph. They landed atop the dike wall battlement.

We crashed back into the water, used our momentum to race along the wall toward where I'd heard the Taxxons. <Now!> Cassie yelled. She opened the whale's mouth again for Jake and Rachel.

<Jake, Aldrea says we have Taxxons,> she warned.

<Yeah, I can smell them,> Jake answered.

Jake and Rachel, a pair of streamlined, dark-gray aquatic creatures with sharply raked fins and a head that seemed squashed and flattened.

<Hammerhead sharks,> Cassie said.

Pah-loosh! Pah-loosh!

<More Taxxons!>

<It doesn't matter. Taxxon versus shark isn't even a battle, it'll be slaughter. None of the Taxxons will live to tell their masters anything.>

<You sound sad.>

<I'm worried for Jake and Rachel. It will be horrible for them.>

"Sreeeeee-yah!"

A Taxxon's scream resonated through the water.

<Worse for the Taxxons, from the sound of it,> I muttered.

<Okay, Aldrea, our turn.>

Cassie had already begun demorphing, building up the smaller, subtler changes so that she could finish in a rush. This part was critical. The humans were determined that the Yeerks never know they'd been on the Hork-Bajir planet.

And yet, Cassie had to be human, at least for a moment between morphs.

It happened quickly, but not instantaneously. We shrank, shriveled, wasted away at a shocking speed. Human arms and legs emerged from the vast tons of blubber.

Whale lungs became human, and Cassie kicked for the surface.

<They'll see you!> I warned.

<Have to breathe,> Cassie said. <Trust my friends.>

Her head, our head, broke the surface. Deep breath. Again. Battle just over our heads atop the dike wall. Two Andalites, tails whipping, slashing, cutting. Hork-Bajir-Controllers backing away and running as one of their own kept yelling "Run! Run! Andalites everywhere! Thousands of them, run!"

Marco, of course.

The Hork-Bajir guards broke and ran. None was interested in a human face poking up from the filthy muck of the pool.

Cassie steadied herself. I felt her exhaustion.

<You're tired.>

<Yeah.>

<It's a miracle you're alive!>

<Yeah.>

She began to morph. Hork-Bajir features appeared, but more slowly now. Too many morphs too quickly. And each a work of art.

As soon as the first blade appeared I said, <Cassie, slam the blade into the wood. It'll help keep you from sinking.>

I heard the sounds of Hork-Bajir-Controllers being rallied above, the shouts and threats of their sub-vissers.

The water echoed with the horrifying screeching of Taxxons.

<We are likely to be overrun within seconds,> Ax said calmly.

<He means, hurry!> Marco cried. <Hurry or we're toast!>

CHAPTER 24

I was fully Hork-Bajir now. I was done for. Tired inside and out.

<Take over, Aldrea,> I said.

Couldn't fight her. Needed her. My mind was going fuzzy, confused. Not sure what body I was in. Bits of unmorphed data, stray instincts, body images, echoes of fins and wings, all jumbled together.

Tseeeew! Tseeeew!

The battle above us on the battlements was joined again.

Aldrea propelled us down, crawling, Hork-Bajir style, down the dike wall, down into the water that no longer rang with the cries of dying Taxxons.

Two hammerhead sharks swam up beside us. There were bits of Taxxon flesh trailing from their rows of razor teeth.

Aldrea was running short of air. We were. She was searching in the murk for some sign on the vast tree trunk before us. Searching . . . the wood was swollen and discolored . . . gasping for breath.

<We're coming in!> Tobias yelled.

Pah-loosh! Pah-loosh! Pah-loosh!

Aldrea said, <Marco! Sink your blades into the wood, don't try to swim! Slow your heart-beats, it will preserve oxygen.>

There! The faint, almost invisible line. It was on the underside of the log, almost where it joined the tree beneath it.

Aldrea slashed with expert ease. Then she pulled.

Nothing!

<The water pressure!> she cried. <Too much. Can't do it!>

Marco crawled down beside us and added his strength.

Slowly the crack widened.

Tseeeeew! Tseeeew! Tseeeeew!

The troops on the battlement were firing into the water. They wouldn't be able to hit us, they couldn't even see us, but they'd soon parboil us.

WOOOOOSH!

The tree opened! Water rushed in, dragging us with it. A tangled mass of sharks, Andalites, and Hork-Bajir was swept inside and bobbed up, to my utter amazement, into air. There was no light, but there was definitely air.

It was silent inside the tree. All the sounds of battle were muffled.

Aldrea gasped, choked, breathed. Then, "Computer, identification: Aldrea-Iskillion-Falan. Code: . . ." She hesitated, then said, "Code: Mother loves Seerow. Ship, acknowledge by turning on exterior lights."

The sudden illumination seemed blinding after the total darkness.

We were floating in a placid pool at the bottom of what looked like an upturned, smooth, wooden bowl. We were inside the tree. Lying half-submerged in water was a stubby Yeerk ship, maybe forty feet long and almost as wide.

We paddled toward the ship and then I felt wood beneath my feet. We stood up.

Jake and Rachel were demorphing as fast as they could, and when they had feet and legs, they, too, stood up in waist-deep water.

"There it is," Aldrea said.

<You have no memory of this ship,> Ax pointed out. <How did you know the identification code?>

"The number represents a logarithm of Seerow's birth date. I always used it."

Jake clapped his hands briskly. "Okay, we have minutes before the Yeerks figure out we're in this tree. Let's get this over with."

We slogged over to the ship and hauled our wet, exhausted selves up inside. I lay on my back on the deck, unable to get up for a while.

"You okay, Cassie?" Rachel asked.

"Aldrea, actually. Cassie is exhausted," Aldrea said.

"Why are you in charge? Get Cassie back!"

Aldrea laughed. "You don't need to worry about Cassie. She takes care of herself quite well."

We stood up and went to the ship's controls. "I need someone on weapons," Aldrea said.

Ax appeared beside her. <We burn our way out?>

"We burn our way out."

<Once we create a hole, the water will rush in and through. It will create a vast drain that will empty much of the pool and suck many of the Yeerks to their doom.>

"Yes," Aldrea said. "Do you object, brother Andalite?"

<No, sister Hork-Bajir. I do not.>

"Then power up the Dracon beams."

The engines began to whine. The Dracon beams began to hum.

<You know, that says something that you can bury one of these things in a tree for years and then just crank her up like this,> Marco said. <Two points for Yeerk technology.>

<"Andalite technology,"> Ax and Aldrea said at the same instant.

"They stole it. That doesn't make it theirs," Aldrea added.

<Everyone should brace themselves,> Ax suggested. <There may be some instability.>

"Ready?"

<Ready.>

"Fire!"

The Dracon beams fired, a blinding blast. And kept firing. A hole burned through the outer side of the tree, out into the air. The water began to rise. The hole grew larger. Now the water was rushing in, gurgling up around the ship. The escaping air howled.

Then, all at once, the wooden wall was gone.

WHAM!

Aldrea hit the engines just as a wall of water caught us, slammed into us, and spit us out into the night.

The ship rolled, spun, bucked then . . .

Whooooom!

<Yeah! Yeah! Yeah!> Marco yelled. <Take that, George Lucas!>

The ship blew out of the log, down the valley, and turned to take a look back. A Bug fighter had come up, saw we were a Yeerk ship, and hesitated.

TSEEEEW! TSEEEEEW!

The Bug fighter blew apart and veered down into the draining Yeerk pool.

Water rushed out of the rapidly widening hole. I could not see the Yeerks, of course, but I knew they were being dragged along in the irresistible current. Hundreds. Thousands. We might never know.

I didn't want to know.

<I sense regret,> Aldrea said. <But this is a great victory. And it is because of you, Cassie. Without you, none of this would have been possible. You've just done the most impossible, incredible, and heroic thing I've ever seen.>

The water continued to drain. The Yeerks in host bodies might be able to save some of their brothers and sisters. Not many. Not all. Thousands of Yeerks would lie there, dying a slow death of dehydration as the water left them stranded, or asphyxiation as they sank, helpless, into the mud.

Because of me.

CHAPTER 25

ALDREA

We delivered the weapons to Quafijinivon. We were reunited with my great-granddaughter, Toby.

The humans, and the one Andalite, had done the impossible, the absurd! But there was no celebration. Instead there were awkward silences and stilted conversations and eyes averted.

I still had charge of Cassie's now-human body. She was doing something very much like sleeping. She had withdrawn, exhausted, depressed.

I drew Aximili aside. "You have lived with these humans. They seem troubled by their victory."

<Yes. They regret doing what they know they must. They have an almost Andalite sensibility.>

I smiled. "I was going to say that they remind me of our Hork-Bajir warriors, who never forgave themselves for learning to kill."

<Let us agree, then, that all civilized species must share a hatred of war,> Aximili said.

"It may be the definition of true civilization," I said. "And yet, we are here to promote another war. The Arn will spawn his new generation of Hork-Bajir, and, thanks to us, they will be armed."

<Young Toby will lead them,> the Andalite said, turning his stalk eyes toward my great-granddaughter.

Toby had her back to us. She had been working with the Arn, learning from him. A strange couple: the last remnant of the race that had made the Hork-Bajir to serve in simplicity and ignorance, and the living example of the Arns' failure.

She was so like Dak when I first met him. Before the battles. Before I had led Dak to serve the Andalite will.

"No," I said suddenly. "No, Toby will not lead them. Her place is with her people, on Earth. Someone, some part of Dak and Seerow and me, will survive to do something besides fighting a war."

<I do not believe she will go voluntarily,> Ax said. <She believes this is her duty.>

"No, I suppose that's true. But with your help, Aximili. And with Cassie's, I think I can convince her." I explained to Aximili. Cassie, of course, heard. And now, at last, she came up out of her haze of regret and guilt.

<You know what this means,> Cassie said.

<Yes. Yes, I know. But my life ended long ago. I tried to pretend otherwise. But with Dak gone, and my little Seerow, and even this planet that I loved so much . . . all that's left now is Toby.>

<No, Aldrea, that's not all that's left,> Cassie said. <You didn't stop the Yeerks. But you slowed them. And that gave humans time. Now we may not stop them, but we, too, will fight, and delay, and weaken them. And someday, somewhere, they will be stopped.>

<And one thing more,> she said. She turned our gaze to Toby. A young Hork-Bajir seer who would, at least in my last dreams, guide her people to freedom.

I almost weakened. It was so hard to say good-bye.

<Let's get it over with,> I said.

<It has been an honor, Aldrea. I still don't know why your *Ixcila* came to me, but it was an honor.>

<Don't you know? Even now? The *Ixcila* is drawn to a mind that reflects it. And I like to think even that inchoate, nonconscious version

of me was honorable enough to know I might be tempted. That I might be tempted to cling to life. And that I might need someone strong enough to return me to the path of my own fate.>

Cassie didn't say anything more. There wasn't anything to say, not to each other.

"Jake!" Cassie cried. "Aldrea is struggling to seize control of me!"

Jake and all the others jerked around, bristling, ready to fight.

Aximili moved quickly to get behind Toby. He whipped his tail forward and held the blade against the young Hork-Bajir's throat.

<Release your hold, Aldrea. You will leave Cassie's body or your great-granddaughter will leave her own.>

"Ax!" Jake cried.

"I'll kill you, Andalite!" I cried through Cassie's mouth. "The Arn will give me a new body and I will come after you!"

<I doubt that, Aldrea, daughter of Seerow the Fool. Toby will go with us as a hostage to ensure your good behavior in the future. Now. Leave our friend Cassie.>

I did. I left Cassie behind, lifted up out of her body, her mind, and was drawn back to the bottle.

I could no longer touch. No longer hear. No longer see.

For a while I could remember.

It wouldn't take Toby long to realize she'd been tricked. But by then Toby and the others would be on their way back to Earth.

My thoughts, my consciousness, my memory, were all fading. I still saw my son. Still saw Dak. Still saw . . .

#35 The Proposal

I haven't decided what I'm going to do when or if I survive this war and actually become an adult. But one thing I know for sure. It won't involve working in a restaurant.

As an Animorph, I've done lots of disgusting things. Heck, I've been lots of disgusting things. But I can tell you, nothing I've done before quite compared to emptying that pig bucket.

It only took a few minutes. But they were the grossest few minutes of my life. Shovels full of chicken bones, half-eaten hamburgers, slime-covered macaroni. All mushed together to make a cold stew more aromatic than a fly's wildest imaginings.

Oh yes. The life of a superhero is a glamorous one.

When I was finished, I raced back into the kitchen from the garbage alley. Waiters and waitresses surrounded the salad station. I squeezed through the throng, looking for the roach-infested, tomato-less salad.

Gone! It was gone!

"Hey," I cried to the salad guy. "What happened to William Roger Tennant's salad?"

He shrugged. "Gone."

"Did you tell the waiter the salad was for Tennant?"

"He can take the tomatoes off if he doesn't like them."

"Aaahhh!"

<Marco?> Jake called out from far away. <Is that you carrying us now?>

I squirmed through the crowd and bolted for the banquet room. Burst through the swinging door. Searched the banquet room for William Roger Tennant.

About twenty round tables covered with white cloths were arranged around the room. And at those tables sat people in tuxedos and fancy dresses and an unusually large number of over-dressed girls my own age or younger.

That would be the Hanson fans.

Against the wall, to the left of the swinging kitchen doors, was a long, rectangular table, raised a few feet off the floor and covered with a long white tablecloth. The dais. Where the guests of honor sat. In the middle of the dais was the podium, from where William Roger Tennant would make his acceptance speech.

<Okay, Marco,> Jake said. <We're being set down now. We'll just have to hope we're where we need to be.>

I sprinted up the few steps of the raised platform. Three guests sat on each side of the podium. William Roger Tennant was seated to the immediate left of the podium. The podium blocked my view of his salad.

The three Hanson kids were to the right of the podium. I sidled up behind them, grinning and trying to look like I was supposed to be there.

<Marco,> Jake called out. <We're moving out.>

I reached Tennant just in time to see him lean over to the person on his left and say, "These tomatoes look delicious!"

"Aaaaahhhhhhhhh!"

The scream came from behind me.

<Uh, that doesn't sound like Tennant,> Tobias said.

<It sounds like Zac!> Cassie cried.

I spun around. Zac Hanson had fallen backward in his chair. His two brothers leaped to his aid.

"Aaaaahhhhhhhhh!" Zac screamed, frantically brushing at the cockroaches in his lap.

"Aaaaahhhhhhhh!" a girl in the audience screamed back.

"Aaaaahhhhhhhh!" Zac yelled.

"Aaaaahhhhhhhh!" cried a woman in a long red dress.

"Aaaaahhhhhhhh!" Within seconds, the room was filled with the sounds of women screaming, chairs overturning, men yelling "Sssshhhh!"

<Run! Outta here!> Jake yelled. Five cockroaches sprung from Zac Hanson's pants and fluttered toward the ground.

<Watch out for the feet!> Cassie cried.

"Aaaaahhhhhhhh!" women and girls screamed.

<That horrible noise!> Ax cried. <Even with this insect's poor hearing I feel as if my head is going to explode!>

<It sounds just like a Hanson concert,> Tobias said.

A cockroach scurried by my foot. I snatched it.

<I have been captured!> Ax cried.

"It's me, man. I've got you," I whispered.

Four roaches shot out of sight beneath the long tablecloth.

<Who's here?> Jake asked. Rachel, Tobias, and Cassie all answered.

<Marco has me,> Ax said, crawling up my wrist.

<Ooookay,> Jake replied. <That could have gone better. Guess it's time for Plan B.>

<Some day when this is all over people will ask us about the war against the Yeerks,> Tobias said. <Let's leave this part out.>

Speak Now or Forever Hold Your Peace.

ANIMORPHS®

K. A. Applegate

Something is driving Marco insane. Something personal. The stress is so bad that it's affecting his ability to morph. The problem? His dad has been dating, and now marriage is on the horizon. Marco knows that his mother might still be alive. But how can he possibly tell his dad the truth?

ANIMORPHS #35: THE PROPOSAL

Visit the Animorphs online at www.scholastic.com/animorphs

Animorphs is a registered trademark of Scholastic Inc. Copyright © 1999 by K.A. Applegate. All rights reserved. Printed in the U.S.A.

ANIT3399

<Know the Secret>

ANIMORPHS

K. A. Applegate

$4.99 each!

- ❑ BBP0-590-62977-8 #1: The Invasion
- ❑ BBP0-590-62978-6 #2: The Visitor
- ❑ BBP0-590-62979-4 #3: The Encounter
- ❑ BBP0-590-62980-8 #4: The Message
- ❑ BBP0-590-62981-6 #5: The Predator
- ❑ BBP0-590-62982-4 #6: The Capture
- ❑ BBP0-590-99726-2 #7: The Stranger
- ❑ BBP0-590-99728-9 #8: The Alien
- ❑ BBP0-590-99729-7 #9: The Secret
- ❑ BBP0-590-99730-0 #10: The Android
- ❑ BBP0-590-99732-7 #11: The Forgotten
- ❑ BBP0-590-99734-3 #12: The Reaction
- ❑ BBP0-590-49418-X #13: The Change
- ❑ BBP0-590-49423-6 #14: The Unknown
- ❑ BBP0-590-49424-4 #15: The Escape
- ❑ BBP0-590-49430-9 #16: The Warning
- ❑ BBP0-590-49436-8 #17: The Underground
- ❑ BBP0-590-49441-4 #18: The Decision
- ❑ BBP0-590-49451-1 #19: The Departure
- ❑ BBP0-590-49637-9 #20: The Discovery
- ❑ BBP0-590-76254-0 #21: The Threat
- ❑ BBP0-590-76255-9 #22: The Solution
- ❑ BBP0-590-76256-7 #23: The Pretender
- ❑ BBP0-590-76257-5 #24: The Suspicion
- ❑ BBP0-590-76258-3 #25: The Extreme
- ❑ BBP0-590-76259-1 #26: The Attack
- ❑ BBP0-590-76260-5 #27: The Exposed
- ❑ BBP0-590-76261-3 #28: The Experiment
- ❑ BBP0-590-76262-1 #29: The Sickness
- ❑ BBP0-590-76263-X #30: The Reunion
- ❑ BBP0-439-07031-7 #31: The Conspiracy
- ❑ BBP0-439-07032-5 #32: The Separation
- ❑ BBP0-590-21304-0 <Megamorphs #1>: The Andalite's Gift
- ❑ BBP0-590-95615-9 <Megamorphs #2>: In the Time of Dinosaurs

Also available:

❑ BBP0-590-03639-4	<Megamorphs #3>: Elfangor's Secret	$5.99
❑ BBP0-590-10971-5	The Andalite Chronicles	$5.99
❑ BBP0-439-04291-7	The Hork-Bajir Chronicles (Hardcover Edition)	$12.95

Available wherever you buy books, or use this order form.

Scholastic Inc., P.O. Box 7502, Jefferson City, MO 65102

Please send me the books I have checked above. I am enclosing $__________ (please add $2.00 to cover shipping and handling). Send check or money order—no cash or C.O.D.s please.

Name______________________________ Birthdate______________

Address____

City_______________________________ State/Zip______________

Please allow four to six weeks for delivery. Offer good in U.S.A. only. Sorry, mail orders are not available to residents of Canada. Prices subject to change. ANI399

http://www.scholastic.com/animorphs

Animorphs is a registered trademark of Scholastic Inc. Copyright © 1999 by K.A. Applegate. All rights reserved. Printed in the U.S.A.

ANIMORPHS®

VISSER

BY K.A. APPLEGATE

The root of all evil took hold here...
It's a story you can't afford to miss.

Invading Bookstores This October.

Visit the Web site at: www.scholastic.com/animorphs

Animorphs is a registered trademark of Scholastic Inc. © 1999 Scholastic Inc. All rights reserved. ANIT3399

ANIMORPHS™

THE ANIMORPHS ADVENTURE CONTINUES ON HOME VIDEO!

Exclusive Never-Before-Seen Footage!

Three Complete Episodes In Each Video!

SCHOLASTIC

©1999 Scholastic Entertainment Inc. Scholastic, Animorphs, and its related characters and logos are trademarks of Scholastic Inc. All rights reserved.

Have you experienced the changes online?

JUN 1 6 2013

ANIMORPHS™

Up-to-the-minute info on the Animorphs!

Sneak previews of books and TV episodes!

Contests!

Fun downloads and games!

Messages from K.A. Applegate

See what other fans are saying on the Forum!

Check out the official Animorphs Web site at:
www.scholastic.com/animorphs

It'll change the way you see things.

Animorphs is a registered trademark of Scholastic Inc. Copyright © 1999 by Scholastic Inc. All rights reserved. AWEB11